Inn Danger

Inn Danger

Dusky Cove Cozy #5

Lori's B&B #5

DI DAVIS

DUSKY COVE BOOKS

INN DANGER © 2019 Dixie Davis

First printing, 2019

Published by Dusky Cove Books

ISBN 978-1-940096-37-7

PRINTED IN THE UNITED STATES OF AMERICA

—For Benjamin
My sweet bear

Chapter 1

Lori Keyes tried not to pace on her porch. The warmth of spring had taken its time in coming, but the weather wasn't the reason she was out here. Neither was the view of the river and the ocean from her bed and breakfast, though she often came out here if she was feeling unsettled. The sight always seemed to bring her peace.

Except today. Because that water was exactly where Mitch was taking her for their "big date." He'd been talking this up for months, and she hadn't had the courage to tell him she didn't like small boats. Even with a life vest, even knowing how to swim, all the rocking and the shaky balance was just too unstable for her liking.

And Mitch had worried she'd be uncomfortable using raw chicken for bait.

Mitch's white SUV pulled around the corner of the Mayweather House to her gravel parking lot. A big green plastic canoe was tethered to his roof.

Oh boy. Her heart seemed to hit her shoes.

Rather than parking over on the side where her guests were, Mitch stopped in front of the steps and bounded out of the driver's seat. "Hey." He gave her a quick kiss. "How's your day been? Guests all checked in?"

Lori could only nod. If she opened her mouth, she wouldn't just report on her guests this weekend—she'd tell him she really didn't want to go.

She *did* want to go. Mitch wanted to do this and she loved Mitch.

She just didn't want to go. Her stomach plummeted too.

"You ready?" he asked.

She nodded again, still not trusting her vocal cords not to betray her true feelings.

Once they were in the car on the way, then she'd be safe to talk. She hoped.

Mitch helped Lori up into the passenger's seat and then got in on his side. At the road, Mitch started the conversation, eyeing the shop across the street from Lori's, Dusky Card & Gift. "You been to see Ray this week?" Mitch asked.

There was a safe topic. "Yes, twice. Why?"

"Katie's having a hard time." Mitch shook his head. He still cared for Ray and Katie Watson, the shopkeepers, like they were his in-laws, though Mitch's wife had passed away a decade ago.

Lori frowned. "I'll bring some breakfast by in the morning after my guests are finished eating."

"And what do your guests have planned?"

She launched into what she knew about her visitors' plans this weekend. The Besases had just come to relax, and Mr. Kirk had asked about fishing excursions.

"Oh, you should've invited him along with us," Mitch said.

Lori glanced at the peak of the canoe's bow in front of the windshield. Two people in a boat was hard enough to balance. How could they possibly fit that many adults in there and not end up capsizing at least once?

She shoved aside the memories of misfortunes at summer camp—every year—and replied to Mitch's comment, which was probably a joke. "Pretty sure he wasn't picturing tying a drumstick on fishing line and hanging out under a bridge. Or catching crabs."

Mitch shrugged. "His loss."

Lori rolled her eyes good-naturedly. "You wouldn't happen to know if Stevie's taking his boat out tomorrow and if he's got any openings, would you?"

"I haven't heard, but I'll ask him."

Mitch drove them out to Miller's Point, a park along the waterfront on the other side of town. Technically, this might not be considered the Cape Fear. It was probably the Intracoastal Waterway. Mitch took the canoe off the SUV, and Lori helped to carry it, loaded with their supplies, down to the tiny dock.

"Are you sure this is a good idea?" Lori asked.

"Of course. You said you like crab, right?"

She sighed. She did like crab—it was one of her favorite foods, but she hardly ever splurged on it. Once Mitch had discovered that, he'd started talking about this trip and had been planning it all winter long.

Lori had to admit it: she was trapped by good intentions. She helped Mitch get the canoe into the water, and he held it steady for her while she stepped in. Lori strangled the sides until Mitch climbed in and launched them off.

Once they were moving over the water—and not moving inside the boat—Lori's rollicking insides calmed down a little. Mitch did all the paddling, but the canoe moved over the water smoothly. The water itself was fairly calm, and at six thirty there weren't many other people out, let alone the barges that usually made their way through here.

Lori let herself relax a little more. This might be nice. The two of them out on the water, enjoying the quiet and the calm and the company. And the crabs. Lori took stock of the equipment on the floor of the boat between them: a bucket to hold the crabs, a net to help catch them, a package of raw chicken drumsticks for bait and a roll of heavy twine for their fishing line. She wasn't a big fisherwoman, but this was definitely the most primitive style she'd ever tried.

But Mitch was certain it would be effective, so she'd let him be the expert.

Mitch guided the boat from the little bay by the park into the Intracoastal Waterway proper. His smooth, even paddling sent them gliding downstream in the wide channel. Slowly, slowly, Lori let go of the canoe's gunwale. Maybe she'd survive this after all.

It wasn't long before they came up on the bridge that led out to the barrier island beyond. Mitch dipped the paddle in the water and slowed them down, guiding them between the last set of pylons and the bank.

Once they weren't moving forward anymore, suddenly Lori felt every little quiver and shake in the boat. This wasn't nearly as safe as she'd thought just a moment ago. Lori grabbed the sides of the canoe again, gripping them hard enough her knuckles turned white. She glanced at Mitch.

He was biting his lip. He'd placed the paddle in the boat, and now that his hands were empty, he was fidgeting.

Maybe she wasn't the only one nervous to be in a boat.

Mitch patted something in his pocket but seemed like he was mostly reassuring himself.

She wished she could do the same.

"You've never been handlining before, right?" he asked.

"I have no idea what that is."

"I'll take that as a yes." Mitch handed her a pair of scissors, forcing her to release the canoe. "Cut two long lengths of twine."

"How long?"

"Very."

Appreciating that oh-so-precise guideline, Lori grabbed the ball of twine and wound off a very, very long piece. She snipped the twine and started over.

"Not that long." Mitch seemed to be holding back a smile. "It just has to reach the bottom."

"I'm sorry, can you see the bottom?"

He checked over the side of the canoe, but Lori already knew the answer. The water was murky enough that you couldn't see farther than six inches, maybe twelve.

Mitch nodded at the twine in her hands. "That's probably good there."

Lori cut the twine again and tossed the ball back into the middle of the boat before returning to her grin-and-grip-it position.

Mitch picked up the package of drumsticks and tore into the plastic. He held up one drumstick. "Tie the handle end on one end of the string."

"Any recommendations on what knot to use, O Wise One?"

He shrugged. "Square, I guess. Needs to hold really well."

Lori barely dared to let go of the gunwale to accept the drumstick. She traded him for the long, long length of twine, then tied her own string tight around the bone end of the chicken leg. "This look good?"

Mitch nodded. "You're a natural."

She rolled her eyes but couldn't hide a smile. Even the silly little things he said like that reminded her of the heady excitement of a new love. Theirs wasn't exactly new—they'd dated by default for a year, then they took a break, and now they'd been dating for real for nearly a year.

Plenty of time to get to know someone enough to fall completely head over heels.

"Toss your drumstick in," Mitch said. Lori took hold of the other end of the string and followed his example. The drumsticks sank, and the lines went slack. They must have hit the bottom.

Lori tucked the twine between her palm and the metal edge of the canoe, still grasping both sides tight. "Now what?"

"The thrilling part of fishing: the waiting."

Normally she would have laughed at that joke. Today, she barely managed a twitter.

"Are you okay?" Mitch asked.

"Of course. Why?"

"Because this boat's not getting any deader, so you can stop strangling it."

Lori laughed and eased her grip on one gunwale. No way was she letting go of both. But she could try to relax. She drew in a deep breath and looked out over the view—the island across the channel, the placid flow of the waterway, the sky just starting to pinken for the sunset, the shadows already beginning to grow longer.

For some reason, tonight the sunset reminded her of another

sunset nearly a year ago, when her son Doug took the love of his life out onto the dock and asked her to marry him.

Right before they discovered she was a serial killer.

So much had changed in the last eleven months. Doug was doing better now, dating again. Her younger son, Adam, had a serious girlfriend and a job close enough to Lori that he visited almost every month. And of course, there was Mitch, the true constant in her universe.

Was she ready for a big change?

Maybe. She was pretty darn sure Mitch wasn't a serial killer, anyway.

Mitch patted his pocket again, then went back to fidgeting.

Mitch never fidgeted.

What was going on? Lori studied her boyfriend's face, the way he absently bit his lip. For someone who didn't want her to be nervous, he was acting pretty nervous himself.

"Lori?" Mitch asked. There was the tiniest little quaver behind the question.

Then the pieces fell into place. Of course there was a reason for this—a reason why he'd insisted on going out on the boat, why it had to be at sunset, why they had to do this tonight. Why he kept patting his pocket.

Was this really happening?

"Yes?" Lori finally managed. She tried to keep the hope out of her voice, but just as surely as Mitch's tone betrayed how he was feeling, hers did the same.

"I think you have a bite."

She furrowed her brow. A bite? What did he mean?

Mitch pointed at the twine clamped between her hand and the edge of the canoe. Oh, of course. Her line was now taut leading to the surface of the water. "What should I do?"

"We want to reel it in very smooth—well, slow enough that he won't let go, but fast enough that he sees his dinner's trying to get away and he better hold on."

Lori had known the chicken legs were for bait, but she hadn't really considered that crabs would be eating the meat. Or that crabs might be carnivores. She started to pull the twine in slowly, trying to find that ideal balance Mitch had referred to. Every couple feet or so, she stopped to make sure the crab was still there, and that sucker tugged on the string, trying to drag his quarry back to his den to eat.

The chicken leg bobbed into sight. Lori lifted the string, pulling the drumstick out of the water. Along with it came a good-sized crab, its blue legs wiggling in the air.

Mitch scooped the dip net underneath the crab. With a little jostling from Lori and Mitch, the crab finally dislodged from its prey.

Mitch brought the net closer to inspect the catch. He gave a low whistle. "Now that's some beginner's luck," he said. "This one's big enough to eat."

"Are there rules about that?"

"Yeah, but you don't need a license to go crabbing by hand, so I don't know if most people follow them." He clutched the bottom of the net and upended it into the bucket. The crab was tangled in the net, but after a shake or two, he dislodged and tumbled out, landing in the bucket with a sharp slap.

Lori leaned forward to peer into the bucket. This was her catch. That sucker had to be the size of her hand. Now that she thought about it, eating crabs made about as much sense as eating spiders. Who had decided to try eating these things? If it was good enough for seals and sea birds, it was good enough for people?

The crab scrabbled up the side of the bucket, splaying its claws at Lori. "Can it get out of there?"

Mitch glanced over. "I don't think so." But the uncertainty in his voice was not what Lori wanted to hear.

The crab slipped, its many legs skritching back down in the plastic bucket. Lori tried not to shudder. She did like the taste of crab, but she wasn't sure she could eat something after she'd looked it in the eyes. Especially after those eyes gave her the heebie-jeebies.

Wherever the eyes were on a crab.

"Ugly things, aren't they?" Lori remarked.

Mitch laughed. "Not everything can be as pretty as you."

She rolled her eyes at the compliment but relished that little bolt of warmth in her belly.

"Was there something you were going to say?" Lori asked. "Before I caught the crab?"

"Oh, um." Mitch bit his lip. "Well—" He looked down at the line in his fingers. It, too, had gone taut, tugging against his hand. "Guess I better reel this in."

Lori nodded, trying not to scowl or sigh. Nerves coiled around her stomach, poised to strike again as soon as Mitch deposited this catch in the bucket.

Was he really going to propose?

Lori almost wanted to drum her fingers as Mitch pulled the twine up. Apparently, he'd let down more twine than he needed, since it seemed to be taking a while.

But Mitch was frowning. "Everything okay?" she asked.

"Yeah, my line's just a little stuck."

"Maybe you caught a tire."

Mitch laughed. "Pretty sure you can't catch a tire with a drumstick."

"Wouldn't put it past you to be the first."

He laughed again, tugging at the line a little harder. "That or I've been attacked by Moby-Crab."

"A definite possibility." She wanted to help, but she couldn't move across the boat to do it. And she seriously doubted that she could do much to help Mitch anyway.

Mitch furrowed his brow, resetting his grasp on the twine for a sharp tug. When it didn't yield, he wrapped each hand in the string to try again. After the second try, the string finally pulled free.

"Did you lose your crab?"

"I'm sure," Mitch said. He pulled the rope a couple inches higher. "Feels like I'm dragging something though. Better get it off there."

Slowly, Mitch reeled in the loose string. Lori watched the

murky water. Something white and blurry materialized in the water, then came into focus as it was towed to the surface.

Fingers.

It was a hand. A human hand.

Lori was too stunned to scream. She turned to Mitch, who'd gone pale.

And then the rest of the body followed, bobbing to the surface. The long, dark hair covered the person's face.

Mitch swore under his breath. "I'm so sorry," he said quickly.

It wasn't her first dead body, not by a long shot—and Mitch knew that.

A ripple of water washed over the body, moving the flowing hair aside to reveal her face. She looked to be around the same age as Lori and Mitch. Her features still looked delicate—perfect. She couldn't have been here very long.

She had on a wedding ring. Lori's heart went out to this woman's family, wherever they were. As awful as this would be for them, at least they'd get closure.

"That's not possible," Mitch breathed.

Lori looked to him. "You okay?"

"No." Mitch stared at the body, his lips pressed together hard enough to lose their color.

Lori waited for him to elaborate. She was used to this—people tended to stop her at the bank and the grocery store to share their life stories with her. All she had to do was wait.

But she waited in silence, Mitch still staring at the body.

Lori knew how to handle this, too—it was time to call the police. She pulled her cell phone from her pocket and dialed 9-1-1. Once the dispatch had her connected to the right city, Lori reported, "We've found a dead body, in the waterway."

Mitch finally tore his gaze from the body. "Oh no, that's not a good idea."

Lori raised an eyebrow—but she couldn't just end the call after making that kind of statement. They'd at least call her back. Lori described their location to Doris, the dispatcher, and she sent the police their way.

"What's wrong with calling the police?" Lori asked as soon as she could.

Mitch drew in a big breath and blew it all out, slumping forward to rest his elbows on his knees. "Because," he said softly. "That's Debra."

He stared at the floor of the boat as he added, "My wife."

Chapter 2

By the time the police had arrived and fished their canoe and their unwanted catch out of the river, it was fully dark. Lori stood on the riverbank, wrapped in a blanket, watching as the cops set up lights and placed the body into a black body bag.

Not just the body. Debra Watson Griffin. Mitch's wife.

Lori understood now why he'd immediately said this wasn't possible.

Mitch's wife had died ten years ago. Hadn't she?

That body had definitely not been in the water ten years. It didn't even look like it'd been in the water a day.

Could she have driven off the end of the road here, plunged into the water, floated free from her car?

Mitch stood five feet away, watching as well. Lori didn't know what to say to him.

This whole time they'd been not really dating and then really dating, he was married. His wife was alive.

Lori shivered. She should have felt cold, she knew, but she just felt numb. As numb as Mitch looked. Was that why he wasn't nearly surprised enough at finding his wife freshly dead?

Two officers kept watch over Lori and Mitch. Perhaps they were there to make sure Lori and Mitch weren't colluding on their story, making sure they covered for one another.

That wasn't a problem. Mitch hadn't said one word to her since he'd said the two that mattered most: "my wife."

He couldn't have done this. Could he?

Two or three other cops worked on securing the scene, keeping the path back to the road clear, and the logistics of hauling the body back up the nearest boat ramp. Another half dozen, some of whom Lori didn't recognize, were in the shallow water, clad in waders, working on sliding the body bag into a litter. Lori had to assume the extra officers were from Caswell Beach or another city on the island across the waterway from Miller's Point. She knew all the Dusky Cove Police.

In fact, the only police officer from Dusky Cove that she *didn't* see was Chief Chip Branson himself.

The officers in the water struggled with the basket but managed to carry the body out of the water, gruesome pall bearers working in reverse, bringing a stranger out of her burial place to try to bring her justice.

Everything about this was backwards. Wrong. Evil.

Even Lori herself couldn't escape that label. She had been dating a married man. Unknowingly, sure, but she couldn't shake the guilt overwhelming her reasoning.

Could Debra have come back to town to reunite with her parents and gone out for a walk first and fallen from the bridge?

Water streamed out of the litter, off the police officers, down the dirt and gravel ramp to the water's edge.

Unlikely.

No matter which way Lori tried to look at it, this looked less and less like an accident.

Finally, the officers bearing the basket reached the relatively level ground of the road, where the medical examiner's van waited, its doors open. The reverse-pallbearers loaded the cage onto the van.

Before they could push the gurney into the van, a gold sedan pulled up flashing police lights. Chief Branson.

Normally, Lori wasn't the happiest person to see him, even more so when she was with Mitch. Chief Branson still had yet to let go of their petty high school rivalry.

A rivalry over a girl.

Lori looked at the body bag on the gurney. Mitch had married his high school sweetheart, beating out Chip Branson for her hand.

The hand that had just floated to the surface of the Intracoastal Waterway—ten years after she was supposedly murdered.

The chief strode over to the officers by the medical examiner's van. "All right," he said, loudly enough for Lori to hear ten feet away. "What have we got?"

The Dusky Cove cops suddenly avoided his gaze, but one of the officers whom Lori didn't recognize stepped up. "Drowning, sir. Victim is a white female around fifty years of age. These two—" He nodded in Lori and Mitch's direction, and the chief spared them a glance before the officer continued. "—found her under the bridge while crabbing. Said their lines got tangled and dragged her up."

Chief Branson looked back at them again, his eyebrows knit together. "Likely story," he called. His words didn't have the usual venom he directed at Mitch, though.

"Chip," Mitch called. "Don't."

Now one of his eyebrows crept higher. Lori couldn't help but echo his skepticism. After how many decades of grief from the man, *now* Mitch would stand up to him?

"Don't look," Mitch clarified.

Lori thought she caught the chief rolling his eyes. Obviously he dealt with worse things than they did on a daily basis—well, relatively speaking. This was Dusky Cove, after all. Lori had personally seen all of the people who'd been killed here over the last two years, too, so she really didn't think Chief Branson's sarcasm was necessary. Before that, they'd gone eight years without a single murder.

Maybe more than eight years. The last victim was supposedly Debra Griffin.

And her death had made Mitch and Chip's feud even more bitter.

"They say the victim's name—"

Ken, one of Lori's favorite officers, stepped up. "Chief, it's probably best if you take a step back right now."

Now his expression turned back to confusion. He turned to the officer who'd given him the run down thus far. "This making any sense to you?"

"No, sir. The decedent is—"

"Really," Lori called to Chief Branson, cutting off the other cop. "Don't do this."

Ken reached for his boss's arm to guide him away, but the chief pulled out of his range. "What are you people talking about?"

Ken shot the helpful loaner officer a look that would have silenced anyone else.

It didn't work on this guy. "It's Debra Griffin."

Chief Branson stared at him as if the name hadn't registered at all. "What did you say?" he finally asked, slowly, carefully, deliberately.

"They say her name is Debra Griffin."

"As in Debbie Watson?"

Finally, the cop cued into the not-even-slightly subtle clues everyone else had been sending, though most likely it was the chief's measured tone—and the fact that he knew her nickname and maiden name—that finally got through to him.

"I'm . . . not sure?" he finished, belatedly tacking on a "sir?"

Chief Branson whirled on the gurney. Ken, Mitch, Lori and a few other officers shouted for him to stop, but the chief didn't listen. He tore open the body bag. From where Lori stood, it seemed like the zipper pull went flying.

For a long, silent moment, the chief stared down into the face of the woman he'd also loved. A woman who he'd lost now for the third time. A woman who clearly hadn't spent the last ten years in the water.

Everything hung still in the air as if suspended in time.

Then Chief Branson turned on his heel, wheeling away from the body. He took in the people around him, the officers, the cars, the lights. Then he marched directly up to Mitch.

Mitch squared his shoulders, ready for the chief's attack. Of course he was. He'd put up with the chief's prejudice for the last decade, and probably much longer, even before Debra had gone missing.

Before Mitch could say anything, the chief pulled back and walloped him.

Lori gasped and automatically lunged for Mitch, but the officer behind her caught hold of her arm before she reached him.

Mitch held his jaw, his wary eyes fixed on Chief Branson. He slowly straightened.

Lori whirled on Chip. "What are you thinking? You can't do that to people! You're the police—the chief of police!"

"It's all right," Mitch said, his voice low. He wiped a thumb across his lower lip. "He's not the chief right now."

Lori looked back and forth between the two of them. Chief Branson was breathing hard, still staring daggers at Mitch. She suddenly got the sense that his badge was the only thing keeping him from trying to beat the tar out of Mitch right this minute.

Mitch, for his part, wouldn't look at the chief. In the past, she'd seen the tension between them, but it was always Mitch who worked to dispel it, to turn the other cheek, to be the bigger person, even if his patience with the other man wore a little thin at times. Today, though, he wasn't being the reasonable one.

He stared at the gravel beneath their feet, looking for all the world one hundred percent guilty.

Mitch couldn't have done this. He couldn't have had anything to do with this. Right?

Lori couldn't answer her own question, and she didn't dare put it to Mitch.

She'd thought she knew this man. She'd thought she wanted to marry him. She'd thought he was a good man, someone she could love, someone she could be safe with, someone she could trust.

Could she really have been this wrong about him?

Lori realized that Mitch wasn't just avoiding Chief Branson's gaze. He was avoiding hers, too.

She turned away. Chief Branson crossed the gravel again to

where the gurney waited. Very carefully, he laid the open flaps of the body bag closed over her face again. Then he gripped the sides of the litter cage.

And the chief of the Dusky Cove Police Department bawled like a baby.

By the time Lori made it home that night, it was after ten o'clock. Her guests' rooms had lights on, which she hoped meant they were home safe. The last thing she needed to do right now was face strangers and pretend like her world wasn't falling apart.

The man she loved was married. Or he had been until his wife had shown up dead that night.

The parlor was, thankfully, empty. Lori trudged over to the blue couch and sank into the cushions.

How would she ever come back from this?

Mitch had been married the whole time they'd dated.

Was this why he'd broken up with her last year? What had changed that he felt like they could date now?

Lori rubbed her temples, but it was her heart that ached.

A knock on the door jolted her from her wallowing. Really, she shouldn't answer. She didn't have to face anyone, and she didn't have the strength to do it either. She drew in a deep breath and prepared herself to not respond.

What if it were the police? She'd already given her statement, and they all knew she didn't know anything.

Of course, the first time she'd found a dead body with Mitch, she hadn't known anything, and the police had arrested her.

She certainly had motive this time around. As Mitch's

girlfriend, why wouldn't she want her rival, his wife, out of the way?

If it was the police, they'd catch up with her whether she answered tonight or not. She had to be sure.

After the third set of knocks—why didn't they just go away?—Lori hauled herself off the couch. She could at least check to see who it was.

She peered through the peephole. Val Cromley stood on her front porch. As if she knew Lori was looking now, Val held up the tray in her hands: one of her famous dark chocolate brownies—a jumbo-sized one from the looks of it.

Lori swallowed a groan. Could she resist the best chocolate dessert in the county at a time like this? No one was that strong.

She opened the door, trying to compose her expression into something neutral and calm.

"Oh, honey," Val greeted her.

That was all it took to break the dam, and Lori burst into tears. Val handed over the brownie and bustled her way inside, closing the door behind her. Val walked her back to the couch and sank down with her.

Lori still wasn't sure she really wanted company—or an audience for her breakdown—but she couldn't send Val away yet. She sniffled, pulling herself together. "I guess you've heard?"

"Yeah." Val squeezed her knee. "I can't believe this."

Lori didn't bother echoing the sentiment. Val must have known Debbie, and she must remember what happened ten years ago, when everyone else in town thought Debbie had been murdered.

Everyone, it seemed, except Mitch, who wasn't all that surprised to see her newly dead.

Before Lori could ask about that time, another knock sounded at her door.

"It's Kim," Val said. Val owned the bakery between the Mayweather House and Kim's Mimosa Café, so it made sense that the gossip train was making its way down Front Street. Once Kim Yates knew, the whole town would know.

Val patted Lori's shoulder, signaling her to stay seated, and Val walked over to answer the door. As she'd predicted, Kim stood on the front porch, a Styrofoam container of soup in her hands.

Kim stepped in without a word and set her Styrofoam on the coffee table, joining Val and Lori on the couch.

Even without them saying anything, Lori felt the strength of having her friends there to support her and sit with her during this time.

"Were you there?" Val asked in a hushed tone.

Lori nodded, picking up the brownie from where she'd left it on the coffee table. Much as she loved Kim's soup, some situations definitely called for chocolate.

And what a chocolate this was. Deep, complex flavor and perfect fudgy texture. Almost enough to make her forget everything that had happened tonight.

But that was only the tip of the iceberg here.

"You know," Lori said, "I've really tried to avoid the rumors and the stories—to the point where I don't even know what happened ten years ago."

Val leaned forward a little to make eye contact with Kim, who returned her grim look. A should-we-tell-her? look.

"At this point, nothing you say could be worse than reality," Lori pointed out.

Kim had to agree with that. "Well, ten years ago, Debbie just disappeared."

Val took a turn when Kim paused. "The last time anyone other than Mitch saw her, the two of them were headed off to the canoe trails together."

The canoe trails? That was where they'd been tonight. Lori tried to suppress a shudder.

"Did everyone think that Mitch killed her?"

Kim fidgeted with the hem of her royal blue blouse. "At first people said it must have been an accident."

"But then, if they'd had an accident while they were canoeing, why wouldn't Mitch have admitted that?" Val shook her head. "Three witnesses saw him coming back from the trails without her."

"Chief Branson was beyond livid."

Val snorted at that. "Understatement of the decade. Rumor has it he spent his life savings funding the divers in the Intracoastal Waterway looking for her body."

"And they never came up with anything?" Lori asked, then popped the last bite of the brownie in her mouth.

Val and Kim both glanced at her, the three of them exchanging a silent *obviously*.

"Does everyone still think Mitch did it?"

"Not *now*," Val muttered. "But I think a lot of people did. Chip, for sure."

Lori pursed her lips. She'd seen his prejudice against Mitch too many times.

"Ray and Katie didn't," Kim added, her voice soft.

How had Lori forgotten her neighbor? Sure, she was in a lot of pain—a *lot*—but this was Ray and Katie's daughter, murdered all over again.

"I tried to stop by," Kim added, "but the lights were off."

Lori hoped they already knew the news—and hoped they would never find out. How much heartbreak could one family endure?

As soon as she was ready, Lori vowed she'd check up on Ray and Katie—and often.

Chapter 3

"So that's the whole rumor?" Lori asked. "The big secret? They supposedly went canoeing and Debbie didn't come back?"

Kim kept her gaze on the Styrofoam container she'd brought and shrugged; Val held out empty hands as if to say she'd given all the information she had.

"Then what did Mitch say? How did he explain coming home alone?"

"He said he'd dropped her off at a friend's house in Caswell Beach. The friend said she went to have her nails done."

Lori shook her head. It certainly looked bad for Mitch ten years ago. "I'm surprised they didn't arrest him."

"Oh?" Val raised an eyebrow. "What makes you think they didn't?"

Lori startled a little. "Mitch never told me he'd been arrested." She would have thought he'd have mentioned it when Chief Branson arrested her for a murder she didn't commit.

Then again, she was dating someone else at the time. Maybe that wasn't something you mentioned to someone who'd hired you to fix a couple things around her inn.

"They couldn't make it stick," Val said. "No evidence, not even circumstantial."

"That was before Chip was even chief," Kim murmured. "Remember who was?"

"Ugh," Val said instantly, "don't even get me started on that man." She shook her head vehemently. "I wish Old Man Branson hadn't retired so early and we could just forget we ever had Chief Lehanneur."

"Where is Chief Lehanneur now?" Lori asked. She'd certainly never met him. Maybe he had a different perspective on the case.

"He moved to Wilmington and was killed in a car accident."

So much for that theory. Lori mentally ran through the roster of the nine policemen in Dusky Cove. Obviously Chief Branson had been on the force at the time. Eddie was too young. Ken might have been. She sorted the other six into those categories, ending up with only four officers who might have been on the force a decade ago.

Then she took a step back from those thoughts. What was she doing? This wasn't her case. She wasn't investigating it. She wasn't formulating a plan, she wasn't interviewing suspects, and she definitely wasn't talking to the police officers who'd worked the original case, period.

She was pretty darn sure Mitch couldn't have killed Debbie today, but she couldn't be his alibi witness, either.

Then again . . . could she be sure he hadn't done this?

Lori thanked Val and Kim for coming over and accepted their hugs, then sent them to their own homes.

She needed to think.

Or better yet, *not*.

The next morning dawned wonderfully bright—for all of two minutes until the reality of last night came crashing down on Lori. She willed herself to get up and put on her favorite, most comfortable knit dress, covered in tiny, multi-colored flowers.

She wouldn't let herself be this upset over Mitch. He obviously wasn't worth her time. Just a year ago, when she'd revamped her entire appearance, Mitch had backed out of their nascent relationship, and she'd tried to convince herself he wasn't worth her time, and here she was again. Heartbroken.

She should have listened the first time.

Now, Lori had the privilege of pretending to be not just all right but bright and cheery with her guests. She painted on a smile and bustled down the stairs.

Mr. Kirk was allergic to wheat, so she'd planned a gluten-free meal for breakfast for the first time. She pulled out the sheet pan, spread aluminum foil over it and put it in the oven to preheat. The leeks and mushrooms were already sliced, waiting in the refrigerator. Once the oven was hot, she tossed the vegetables with olive oil and let them sauté in the oven.

All right, maybe that didn't *really* count as sautéing, but she'd definitely give herself a break this morning.

Once the leeks were tender, Lori added the mixed greens, letting the heat of the pan wilt the kale and collards. She'd never had kale before, so this was definitely a risk.

The greens began to wilt. Lori changed the oven to broil, then made little nests in the greens. She cracked an egg into each nest, then slid the pan back into the oven to finish cooking the eggs.

She hoped the yogurt parfaits, fruit salad and muffins would round out the meal enough—though obviously Mr. Kirk couldn't have any muffins. Lori added tiny milk cartons in a bowl of ice to the serving table, then pulled out the eggs in greens and set them in the chafing dish.

Another pan of sausage patties and breakfast was ready.

Two years in, and she was finally getting the hang of breakfasts—especially options that required little effort when your mind kept fleeing elsewhere.

Even when you really, really didn't want it to.

Lori tried to shake off that thought, cleaning up the kitchen and setting out the breakfast dishes to keep her mind off the horrors of the night before.

She still couldn't wrap her mind around what had happened. Everyone thought Debbie was dead, and had been for a decade, and then her body suddenly surfaced—literally—here in Dusky Cove again?

"Good morning," a voice rang out across the dining room.

Lori hurried to pull out of her tailspin of memory and deposited the basket of silverware on the serving table. She turned around to find Manuel Besas standing in the doorway. "Morning." She made herself smile back, although in all honesty, it would have been hard *not* to return Manuel's infectious grin, he was so young and full of life.

He stepped in the dining room, his wife trailing behind him, her smile just as bright, but somehow more soothing, her fair complexion a contrast to her husband's deeper skin tone. "Good morning, Mrs. Keyes," Chelsea Besas bid her.

"Call me Lori." She gave a tour of the breakfast options for the morning, then invited them to dig in.

Manuel and Chelsea began filling their plates. "Any news?" Manuel called over his shoulder to Lori.

The smile on her face froze, and she couldn't find words to answer.

Chelsea was scooping yogurt into a tall glass. She set down the spoon to pat her husband on the shoulder. "We don't want to hear about the news, dear. We're on vacation!"

Lori joined in their laughter, though her voice sounded too high pitched to herself. Hopefully the Besases wouldn't notice.

She chatted with them over breakfast, recommending some of the more relaxing activities in the area: the ferry to Bald Head Island, the Salt Marsh Boardwalk, any of the beaches. Chelsea voted for the beach, and Lori promised to loan them a picnic basket with a cooler inside for the day.

They were already on their way upstairs to get ready when her other guest came down. Lori showed Mr. Kirk around the breakfast table, and he thanked her for the gluten-free options. He settled at a table. He'd seemed . . . quiet to Lori Thursday at check-in, and a good night's rest hadn't changed that.

Lori headed to the breakfast table and ventured to attempt a conversation anyway between Mr. Kirk's bites of eggs and yogurt. "Are you still thinking about going fishing?" Lori asked.

Mr. Kirk jumped, and Lori kicked herself for breaking the silence. She could have at least waited until she sat down at the table so she didn't scare the poor man out of his skin.

"I . . . I'm not sure," Mr. Kirk said at length. "I'm pretty tired."

Lori nodded sympathetically, though she was pretty sure this man, who couldn't even be forty yet, had *not* spent the night tossing and turning because the person he thought he was going to marry might actually be a would-be bigamist or a murderer or both.

Mr. Kirk finished off his eggs. "I'm kind of thinking of calling it a weekend and checking out early. Not sure I feel like staying."

"Oh, dear—is there anything I can do to help?" Lori hoped she hadn't already done too much. Hopefully *she* wasn't the reason he wanted to leave.

He shook his head. "I don't think so."

"How about a nice, quiet morning in? You could get some rest. The best part of any vacation."

Of course, Lori couldn't remember the last time she'd gone on vacation all by herself. Maybe a quiet morning in would just make him feel lonelier, especially if he'd left his family behind to come here.

Lori subconsciously checked Shawn's left hand for a wedding ring. His ring finger was bare, but if she squinted, Lori could imagine she saw a ring tan line.

Oh, goodness. He wasn't vacationing after a recent divorce, was he? That sounded like a recipe for failure.

Maybe he needed the distance from his problems at home. And what better way to forget all that than to get lost in a book or a movie? "We have a collection of videos," Lori suggested. "And some really great reads."

"I dunno." Mr. Kirk poked at his yogurt with his fork. "I should probably go home."

Lori bit her lip. "I'm so sorry, but we do have a cancelation policy."

Mr. Kirk looked up. "Nobody leaves a vacation early, do they? That's weird."

She couldn't tell if he was mocking her or asking her. "If you really feel like you don't want to be on vacation, there's nothing stopping you from leaving. But we have you booked through Tuesday, and I'm afraid I would have to charge you." She couldn't lose her longest booking. She'd never be able to fill it at the last minute.

But Lori's stomach constricted. She really hated bringing her policies down on people, though she knew they were there to protect her and her business. She literally couldn't afford to *not* enforce them. Mr. Kirk nodded, his gaze on the pink blob of yogurt he was spreading across his plate.

"Would it help to talk about it?" Lori offered gently. On a weekly basis, people seemed to bare their souls to her about their deepest trials. She was used to it—so much so that when someone held back, she was almost worried she was losing her touch.

Mr. Kirk forced a wan smile. "Not unless you can undo the past."

Lori's return smile was as thin as her guest's. "Afraid not."

And there were plenty of things she'd change about the last two years.

The last two days.

Most of all, if she could go back and change the past, she'd do whatever it took to stop the six—now seven—deaths she'd investigated.

Not that she was investigating Debbie's death. At least not her actual death.

Didn't she want to know what had happened?

Mr. Kirk stood, gathering his plate. "I think I'm going to . . . go for a walk."

Lori stood also, though she hadn't even started on her egg. Small wonder Mr. Kirk didn't want to talk to her—she'd obviously been too lost in her own thoughts to be a good hostess. "Mr. Kirk—"

"Shawn."

"Shawn." She grinned, more warmly this time. "Please, if there's anything I can do to make your stay more enjoyable."

He just laughed—a sad, bitter sound. "I was hoping I could come here to forget my problems. So please forgive me if I don't want to delve into them right now."

"Of course." Goodness, she was really blundering this morning. "I'm here if you ever need anything."

Shawn nodded weakly. "Thanks." He retreated from the dining room. Lori leaned into the parlor to watch him go, passing the Besases on their way down, ready for a day at the beach.

"Let me get your basket!" Lori called as they reached the front door. She ducked into the kitchen and returned to the front room with a stocked basket.

Manuel and Chelsea were talking to someone on the front porch. Lori crossed the parlor to see who was here.

She was almost to the door when she realized she was expecting to find Mitch standing there.

Not just expecting. Hoping.

Lori chided her silly heart and maneuvered behind Chelsea to find Andrea Hopkins, the curator of the Dusky Cove Museum, standing on the front porch. She wore a pantsuit that was halfway between artistic and business-like, and her hair, normally styled in short braids with beads, was free in a natural Afro.

"Hi, Andrea," Lori said, handing over the picnic basket to the Besases. "My guests are headed out to relax on the beach all day."

"That sounds so nice," Andrea cooed, stepping aside to let the Besases past. With farewell pleasantries out of the way, Lori showed Andrea in.

"I heard what happened," Andrea said immediately. "Obviously." She opened her arms and gave Lori a tight hug.

Andrea had always been on Lori's side, from the time she'd arrived in town and was almost immediately framed as a murderer. To have her oldest friend in town here, to support and love her, got Lori started on the tears again.

"Oh, sweetie," Andrea held her at arm's length. "I wish I came with better news."

Lori wiped her eyes. "News?"

Andrea always had news. Her husband was the editor of the town newspaper. Kim might be the gossip queen, but Andrea was the one who had all the facts.

Judging by the grim look in Andrea's eyes, today it looked like those facts weren't good. At all. Andrea took a seat on the couch and a deep breath as if bracing herself, and Lori followed suit.

And then completely lost her nerve. "You lived here ten years ago, didn't you?" Lori asked, cutting off whatever Andrea was going to say.

"I—what?" Andrea caught up to the abrupt subject change quickly. "Yes, we lived here ten years ago."

"When Debbie died—they thought she did, I mean?"

Andrea was already a step ahead of her again. "I remember it, yes."

"What did Curtis put in the paper then?" Curtis was a stickler for facts and fact-checking. The *Dusky Chronicle* might be a small-town newspaper, but they held to journalistic standards. Even when that meant reporting Lori's arrest two years ago.

"Well." Andrea's dark eyes rolled upward, like she was flipping through her memory. "Curtis tried to tread very carefully with that one. Obviously he didn't want to get on Chief—well, Detective Branson, back then—didn't want to get on his bad side. Chip is still one of Curtis's most important sources."

Lori nodded. One of Curtis's best sources who conveniently leaked whatever he wanted people to think. Most of the time, Curtis was good about seeing through Chip's spin on things.

But could anyone see through ten years of suspicion?

Lori focused on the scrolling yellow oak leaves on her historical replica wallpaper. Wallpaper her friend—now murdered—had found for her. Wallpaper her boyfriend—now a murderer?—had installed for her. "Do you—or did you—think that Mitch killed Debbie?"

Andrea pressed her lips together, her gaze sliding to the side.

"I didn't want to think it, but . . . I couldn't come up with any other explanation."

"And now?"

"Now I don't know what to think."

Lori folded her arms, more giving herself a hug than anything. "That makes two of us."

"Well, someone else does know exactly what he thinks."

Lori, for one, didn't know what Mitch could be thinking now. Normally, they would have talked about it, but he was giving her a wide berth, apparently.

But Andrea would only be saying that if she or Curtis had spoken to him. "Fine," Lori said, a little more pique than she'd like in her voice. "What does Mitch have to say for himself?"

"Mitch?" Andrea pulled back. "I meant Chief Branson."

Lori tried not to roll her eyes. Everyone in town knew what Chief Branson must think, even if they hadn't watched the chief punch Mitch or sob over his high school sweetheart's body. "Chief Branson thinks Mitch is responsible," Lori supplied. "Just like he does whenever anything goes wrong in town." Everything up to and including the hit-and-run accidents a year ago were supposedly Mitch's fault.

Although this case actually did seem to have a connection to him, one that even Lori wouldn't try to deny.

"Yes," Andrea finally said. "And that's why Mitch is in jail now."

Chapter 4

Lori simply stared while Andrea's words echoed in the parlor. How could they have already arrested Mitch? It wasn't even nine o'clock yet.

Chief Branson obviously moved quickly when he thought he had a suspect. She'd already learned that the hard way.

On the other hand, if he believed Mitch was guilty, he should have just arrested him last night instead of slugging him.

Lori found her hackles rising at the memory of the chief of police hitting the man she loved—had loved. Obviously this wasn't Mitch's fault.

But Mitch had just taken the hit.

As if it *was* his fault.

Lori realized she was pacing around the blue couch, where Andrea had settled like she was here for the long haul.

"What do you think, Andrea?"

"I don't know what to think. Debbie Griffin, back from the dead, but now *actually* murdered?" The full weight of the truth seemed to fall on Andrea. "I don't know what happened ten years ago," Andrea admitted. "But I know I want to find out."

Lori nodded slowly, but she didn't know how deep that feeling went for her. Yes, this was obviously a puzzle that wanted puzzling out, but that didn't mean Lori wanted to be the one to tease out the truth.

Could she handle finding out any more of his secrets? She just wanted space. Peace. Quiet.

Lori glanced at the cream-colored ceiling above her. Sounded familiar.

She turned back to Andrea. "Are you going to investigate then? You and Curtis?"

"Of course Curtis is. That's his job."

Right. Lori sank down onto the couch next to Andrea.

"Someone I know has a pretty good track record for solving murders."

For a split-second, Lori perked up at the prospect of someone else—a neutral party—who could help Mitch. But then she turned to Andrea and saw in her eyes exactly whom she meant: Lori.

Yes, Lori had solved a few murders. That didn't mean she could figure this one out. Or that she wanted to.

"I'm too close to it, Andrea," Lori said softly.

Andrea put her hands over Lori's, clasped in her lap. "That's okay. You're not the hall monitor of Dusky Cove. It's not your job to investigate every time."

Tears threatened again, and Lori blinked quickly. "I'm still worried about him," she admitted.

Andrea squeezed her hands. "Whatever you're feeling is okay. You're allowed to feel that way. Whether you want to help Mitch or even if you think he did this."

Did she think he'd done this? Sure, he had motive—a lot of motive. She could probably think of four or five reasons she would have wanted Debbie dead if she were in Mitch's shoes. All that he'd endured when she went missing, the mere fact that she'd abandoned him or possibly even framed him, her showing up again when Mitch was finally ready to move forward with Lori. . . . Lori didn't exactly love her for all those reasons, too.

Andrea patted her shoulder. "I'd hate for you to judge him without hearing his side of the story."

"What *is* his side of the story?" Lori didn't dare to hope that Curtis had managed to squeeze in an interview with Mitch before Chip arrested him.

"I don't know." Andrea furrowed her brow, her lips twisting together as she pondered the question. "I guess what I'm saying is that we can't jump to conclusions."

It was hard not to do some serious leaping when you were the one who'd discovered the body.

On the other hand, why would Mitch have taken her to the exact spot—or downstream from the exact spot—where he'd just drowned his estranged wife? That would require either supreme arrogance or supreme idiocy. And the Mitch she knew didn't have either of those qualities.

But the Mitch she knew wasn't real. The Mitch she knew wasn't a liar; he wasn't married; he wasn't a murderer.

"If it were anyone else," Lori murmured. "Anyone else—you know I'd already be down at the police station or the jail or interviewing somebody."

Andrea nodded. "If it were anyone else, you'd have no trouble working to find out the truth."

"Andrea, nobody wants the truth more than I do. Nobody deserves it more than me. But that doesn't make me the right person to go out there and try to find it."

Andrea lifted a skeptical eyebrow, but Lori's tone was final. This was all she could handle, reeling from everything Mitch had put her through. She thought he was innocent—she needed him to be innocent—but her emotions were just too raw to be the one to go out and prove it.

"I didn't know Debra well," Andrea admitted, her gaze turning to the dormant fireplace. "And I do like Mitch. But most of all, I want to know what happened. Yesterday, and ten years ago."

Lori frowned at that phrasing of the problem. She wanted to know the truth too—she deserved it more than anyone, except maybe Mitch.

And then it hit her: all this time, she'd been so focused on herself as a victim here because of what this death meant. But Mitch hadn't purposefully been philandering. He was as much a victim of Debra's deception as she was.

Andrea stood, straightening the flowing edges of her suit jacket. "Good luck." Andrea held out her arms for another hug, which Lori gladly accepted.

Having her friends stand by her right now was all she could ask—and it was probably all that was going to get her through this experience.

Andrea left to head into work at the museum, while Lori busied herself cleaning up breakfast. Only a little of the yogurt was left, so she scooped it into a shallow Tupperware container to freeze it for homemade frozen yogurt, one of Mitch's favorites.

Lori caught herself and pivoted to scrape the yogurt directly into the trash can. The last thing she needed right now was to leave herself reminders of him in her own freezer.

And not just because she felt guilty for taking a step back from probably the most important murder investigation Dusky Cove would ever see.

Lori poured the granola into a bag and resealed it. She carried the chafing dishes into the kitchen, wrapped up the leftovers for future lunches and dinners, washed the dishes. She did *not* think about Mitch sitting in the same prison where she'd had to spend a weekend.

She worked so hard to *not* think about him, Lori not only washed the serving dishes and plates from breakfast by hand, she scrubbed the stainless steel kitchen counters, mixed up a batch of sweet roll dough for tomorrow, started her daily load of linens, switched out the dining room tablecloths, and deep cleaned the parlor. It wasn't until she was dragging the refrigerator out of its slot in the racking that Lori finally accepted what she was actually doing: merely avoiding the real stress in her life.

Avoiding the heartache.

Cleaning had always been her go-to method of dealing with stress. But even that didn't seem like enough this time around.

Her house had been spotless for months after her husband Glenn died all those years ago. Finally, she'd seen a therapist and started actually healing.

Somehow, this was so much more traumatic than slowly losing her husband to cancer, as awful as that had been.

Lori forced herself to push the fridge back where it belonged.

She still needed to feel productive, so she chopped up vegetables for an omelet bar tomorrow. If she still had guests once the news got out about Debra.

Once again, she worked very hard—literally—to keep her mind off what was troubling her. Though slicing up the peppers and onions and mushrooms didn't do much to keep her mind off the hand floating to the surface, the horror—but not shock—on Mitch's face, the way he let Chip punch him.

This wasn't fair. Not any of it. After being alone for so long, after the ups and downs Mitch had put her through, after they'd finally both found some happiness, everything had to come crashing down now? What had she done to deserve this?

Lori shook her head at herself and the mountain of sliced veggies she'd built. She grabbed a large Tupperware tub and started piling the vegetables in there. She'd learned long ago that what a person "deserved" had nothing to do with what they got in life. Being a good person, having the good fortune of being born in a certain place, time or social standing, even hard work weren't guarantees that your life would be easy and good forever.

Death came to everyone, didn't it?

And it had come to Debra Watson Griffin twice.

Lori stopped short and turned around. Out her windows, she stared at the shop across the street, also in a converted historic home. Dusky Card and Gift's windows were dark. The "Closed" sign hung askew on its door.

Debra didn't deserve whatever had happened to her, no matter what she'd done to Mitch. But most of all, Ray and Katie, her parents, didn't deserve this.

Here Lori had been, wallowing in her self-pity, griping about what she "deserved" and how she was the real victim here. There had actually been a *murder*, with a real *victim*. Her parents were some of Lori's closest neighbors, who'd always been kind and supportive to her.

Those were the real victims.

Even if her heart was too caught up in her relationship with Mitch and its demise—maybe?—to work the case for him, and even if her personal feelings about Debbie's disappearance and dramatic reappearance were too hard to work the case, she could do this for her friends who had just lost their only daughter all over again.

She had to.

Lori gathered her courage about her. She could do this for Ray and Katie. Even if she'd only barely met Katie after two years of living across the street. The woman was bedridden, so it wasn't as though she was avoiding Lori.

As a good Southern woman, Lori couldn't just go over to a home of a grieving friend empty-handed. Just like Val and Kim had done for her last night, she had to bring more than just an offer to help.

Lori flipped through her favorite cookbook until something jumped out at her: strawberry sweet rolls. Ray had mentioned once that Katie loved strawberries. This would be perfect.

The dough was already risen—a little over proofed, perhaps. Lori punched it down and got out her rolling pin. She tried not to take too many of her frustrations out on the dough—speaking of things that didn't deserve cruel treatment.

Once it was rolled out in a large rectangle, Lori fetched the strawberries and strawberry jam from the fridge. Much as it pained her to spend the money on fruit that was out of season—and therefore not very good—Lori had found that having a special treat seemed to make her guests especially happy.

Although it hadn't worked for Shawn. But, then, who could be happy if they could never eat another baked good as long as they lived?

As if Lori didn't have significant problems. Whatever Shawn was going through had to be serious, too, at the very least to him.

Lori warmed up the jam to make it gooier, then spread it over the dough. She quickly chopped up the strawberries and spread them over top of that, then rolled up the dough just like a cinnamon roll. Once they were risen, Lori slid the rolls into the oven.

Baking was supposed to make her feel better. She wasn't sure it was working.

Then again, maybe it was the *eating* that actually cheered her up.

The timer rang, and Lori pulled the rolls out of the oven. She spread the cream cheese frosting—store-bought, though she'd keep that secret to herself—over the top, letting the tangy sweetness melt into every spiral and nook.

Both pans, one unfrosted, went on the tall kitchen rack to cool. Lori hurried upstairs to try to make herself look presentable. Even her favorite dress wasn't doing much to make her feel happy, and the bags under her eyes betrayed the tossing and turning she'd endured the night before.

She could hardly imagine Ray and Katie had had an easier time of it, though.

Lori fluffed her curls, leftover from yesterday, and pulled out her makeup.

Did she dare apply any? She didn't have waterproof mascara or eyeliner, and she couldn't imagine her meeting with Ray and Katie was going to be happy.

She changed her mind and put the makeup away. She quickly straightened her quarters, putting away the things she hadn't had the energy or time to the night before. The special occasion makeup she only wore on a date with Mitch. The muddy shoes she'd taken off. The bed she'd tried unsuccessfully to sleep in.

Lori shook off the self-pity. She was going to be there for Ray and Katie. They probably knew how much she was hurting, too. But she hadn't had one of her children fake her own death and pretend like she didn't exist for a decade, only to actually show up dead.

Murdered?

It was hard to say. An awfully big coincidence either way.

Unless this really was all related.

Lori headed back down to the kitchen and covered the smaller, frosted pan of strawberry rolls with foil. The frosting had already begun to set up again, a little more translucent than before, showing the beautiful swirls through the glaze.

Normally, Lori would have been thinking of saving one for Mitch about now. Lucky for her, she didn't have to worry about that anymore.

Lori was halfway across the street when it hit her. Not only had the Watsons lost their daughter all over again, but since Debbie had been gone, Mitch had still been like a son to them.

And now they were losing him, too.

She definitely wasn't the biggest victim.

Chapter 5

The lights were off inside Dusky Card and Gift. Lori peered through the windows. Somehow, without Ray there to liven the place up, it really did look like the town joke of "Dusty" Card and Gift.

Lori had loved the little shop with its unique finds—historical, authentic, local, touristy and all combinations of the above. But she'd never fully realized that her favorite part of the shop had to be Ray himself.

She knocked on the door, the "Closed" sign rattling against the glass. She didn't expect Ray, and especially not Katie, to answer.

Luckily, Lori knew what to do. Obviously neither their daughter nor their surrogate son was around to take care of them, so Lori figured she must be third in line. After all, three months ago when Mitch was in Atlanta for a botany seminar and Ray had taken Katie to Duke Hospital for surgery, Lori was the one who was in charge of watering houseplants and accepting deliveries.

And that meant she knew where the spare key was. Lori rounded the house to the back porch and felt underneath the porch steps. Mitch had installed powerful magnets underneath the side of the treads to hold an extra key. Lori slid it sideways off the magnets and climbed the porch steps to unlock the back door.

"Ray?" she called. "It's me, Lori."

The kitchen was dark and silent.

Were they not up yet? Or just not up to getting up yet?

Lori let herself in and turned on the lights. She knew all too well that some tragedies were so hard to face that sometimes it was just easier to go back to bed.

But she also knew that those true tragedies were always the ones that wouldn't go away with a little more sleep.

She set her strawberry rolls on the counter and put a pot of coffee on. Even if Ray and Katie couldn't provide their own sense of normalcy, Lori would do what she could to keep their world turning.

"Who's there?" Ray's voice carried down the stairs, little more than a weak croak.

"It's me, Lori," she called back. Again.

Halting steps creaked down the stairs. "Do you need something?" Ray asked.

She turned around to face him as he reached the tiny kitchen. His threadbare bathrobe hung limp on him, as if he'd lost twenty pounds overnight. His always dull blue eyes seemed even weaker somehow now, as if they were fading away even faster than he rest of him.

He'd aged at least a decade in the last twenty-four hours. Lori couldn't exactly blame him.

"I'm sorry to bother you," she said gently. "I just wanted to make sure you two were all right."

"All right?" Ray clenched his jaw, taking a step forward to clamp a hand on the back of one of the kitchen chairs. "My daughter comes back from the dead just long enough to get herself killed and you want me to be all right?" By the time he reached the last word, he was shouting.

Lori took his anger like a wave breaking over her. "Of course not. You don't ever have to be all right after something like this. I just brought you some breakfast."

Ray instantly deflated. "I'm sorry, it's just—" He shook his head, wiping his eyes.

"Nobody knows how to deal with death," Lori said, her voice gentle.

"You'd think it'd get easier with practice."

Lori fixed him with a look that said *really?* "I think this is one thing that practice can't make perfect."

Ray shuffled over to the kitchen table and sank into a chair. Lori grabbed a napkin from the holder decorated with a wooden goose silhouette and used it to serve Ray a strawberry roll. "Is Katie awake?"

"Yes."

"Should I take her one?"

"Sure." Ray settled with his elbows on the table on either side of the strawberry roll, staring down on it like it held the depths of his soul.

Or the past.

Lori grabbed another napkin and pulled another strawberry roll from the pan. She climbed the stairs and headed to what she hoped was the master bedroom. She didn't think she'd ever been upstairs in their apartment. Usually she stayed in the storefront or the kitchen.

The upstairs was quiet. Eerily so. There were only four doors off the hall and one clearly was a closet, so she had a pretty good chance of finding Katie on her first try.

Lori crept down the carpeted hall. The closer she got to the door at the end of the hall, the stronger the smell of medical disinfectant grew.

Lori opened the door slowly, a loud creak emanating from the hinges. "Miss Katie?" she whispered.

"Who's there?" Katie's thin voice carried a note of pain.

From whatever it was that had kept her bedridden for years, or from the turn of events from last night? Lori poked her head in. "Hi, Miss Katie. It's me, Lori, from across the street?"

Katie lay on the bed, her oxygen tube loose, her wispy white hair disheveled. Lori had only seen her once or twice, but she'd always had her hair carefully combed back into a neat ponytail. "Hi, Lori. What can I do for you?"

Lori couldn't hold back a sad chuckle. Everything that Katie was going through, and her first thought was what she could do for Lori? "Nothing, Miss Katie. I was just bringing you some strawberry sweet rolls."

"Oh. Thank you." But she didn't perk up at the mention of the treat. Her gaze shifted past Lori, first to the window and then to nothing.

Lori crossed the room to the hospital bed where Katie lay. "How are you holding up?"

"Not as well as I would've thought," Katie murmured. "You'd think that you couldn't hurt anymore after ten years of dealing with this. I thought I'd be used to it." She shook her head slowly.

Lori set the strawberry roll on the high table beside her bed. "There's no instruction manual for mourning."

"And if there were, I don't think they'd cover this situation."

"Kind of a special case," Lori agreed.

"You know," Katie said, although it sounded like she was talking more to herself than Lori, "when Chief Branson came by, I knew something had to be wrong. Of course. Chip's never made many social calls. But when he said they'd found Debbie, I thought they meant they'd finally found her body after all these years. He had to tell us what he was saying at least three times before it started to make sense. Something like sense."

Nothing like sense, really. "Yeah, I was there, and it doesn't make any sense to me."

Katie's laugh was completely humorless. "No, I suppose it doesn't."

"I know this is a difficult time for you, but I'd love to help you however I can."

"You're the resident sleuth, aren't you?"

Lori turned one palm skyward, the weakest possible shrug. "I guess I am."

"Then I want you to figure this out. If Mitch did this." Her voice hitched on her former son-in-law's name, and she took a deep breath. "Or who else did."

"Of course. For you."

The faintest shadow of a smile passed over Katie's countenance. "Strawberry roll?" she said after a moment.

Lori quickly handed her the treat from the table. She realized she didn't know if Katie could feed herself—she'd brought plenty of treats and meals over the years, but Ray always brought them up to her.

Katie quickly settled the matter by taking the roll and napkin from Lori's hands. "Thank you."

Lori nodded. She hated to bring it up just when it seemed like Miss Katie was finding some small measure of peace for a moment, but she'd just asked Lori to investigate. Plus, Lori wasn't likely to find herself in this room again for a while, if ever.

"Miss Katie," she started slowly, "what do you remember about what happened ten years ago?"

"The first time my daughter died, you mean?"

So much for putting things delicately. "Yes."

Katie sank back further into her pillow as if merely thinking of that time made her weaker, looking toward the heavens. "Debbie was unhappy. She tried to hide it, but if you knew her well, you could see it."

"Unhappy in what way?"

Katie's gaze fell from the ceiling to the strawberry roll in her hands. "I must be the worst mother in the world, but I don't know. I tried to talk to her about it, but . . . she just never seemed to want to open up to me."

"Did she confide in anyone else? Ray? Mitch?"

Katie shook her head. "I don't know. Ray's never admitted it if she did. It was always hard to talk about Debbie with Mitch after everything he went through."

"I heard he was arrested."

Katie tore off a corner of the sweet roll and a bit of strawberry tumbled out onto the napkin. "He was. Spent a couple weeks in jail until he came up with bond."

Lori winced inwardly. A single weekend there was enough to scar a person for life—as Lori knew too well. Adding on losing your wife and being falsely accused?

And now Mitch was back there.

"Did you think that he did it?"

Katie plucked the strawberry bits from her napkin and put

them in her mouth. "I didn't know. I didn't want to believe it. Mitch had never seemed capable of it. He was more bewildered than guilty. And sad. Awfully sad for a person who'd supposedly killed her."

Lori concentrated on her fingernails. She didn't have a ton of experience with murderers, but it seemed to her that being sad could also be a side effect of killing someone. Regret.

"Did you think she was still alive?"

Katie's blanket over her chest rose and fell with a deep breath. "I couldn't imagine her being dead. But how could she just drop off the face of the earth like that? She never called or wrote or emailed ever, not even to say, 'Hey, Mom, I'm still alive.'"

"Do you think she knew what a controversy she'd caused?"

Katie took another bite of the roll portion of the strawberry roll. "I don't think she knew, but maybe she did. Maybe she wanted that? Maybe she meant for Mitch to suffer? All she had to do was drop a postcard in the mail, for heaven's sake. Not one word—for ten years?"

Unlike most people, Katie didn't raise her voice as she fell deeper and deeper into the sorrowful sermon. Instead, her voice grew softer, almost a whisper by the time she finished. As if the anger was wearing her out right in front of Lori's eyes.

She had a decade's worth of anger built up. Of course it was burning right through her. Lori couldn't fault her one bit.

Lori tried again. "I'm guessing you didn't know anyone who did have contact with her during that time?"

"As far as I know, the whole town was pretty convinced she was dead."

"Including Mitch?"

Katie nodded, pausing to chew another bite of the strawberry roll. "You know, my memories aren't the sharpest from that time—it was right before I took sick."

Lori still had no idea what specifically ailed Katie, but obviously it was fairly serious if she'd been bedridden for a decade.

Katie fell into silence, picking at her strawberry roll. "Would you like a drink?" Lori asked.

Katie pointed at a tall glass of water on the table. "I'm just fine, thank you. Why don't you head down and keep an eye on that husband of mine? He's liable to act out."

Lori laughed, but she had to wonder whether Katie was serious. Had he done something rash the first time they'd lost their daughter?

Lori headed back down the stairs to the kitchen. Ray didn't seem to have moved, though the strawberry roll in front of him was gone.

"Feast or famine," he murmured as Lori settled at the table next to him. "Either you're too upset to eat or too upset to stop."

Lori cast a meaningful glance at the other two rolls in the pan, but she assumed they were still there. Ray didn't look up to catch her joke.

"Ray," she said gently, "Miss Katie wants me to look into this. What do you want?"

A fist slammed down on the table, and Lori jumped. "I want my daughter back." His voice was low, almost menacing.

"I wish I could give you that." Lori slowly reached for his hand, giving him plenty of time to pull away if he wanted. He let her rest a hand on his forearm. "But since I can't, I want to do what I *can*. What I've done for other people."

Ray buried his face in his other hand but nodded.

"Can you help me understand the background a little more? Katie said her memory of that time is a little off because she took sick."

Ray nodded. "Yes, because of the stress, the doctor said. Tripped a switch in her system we're trying to reset."

Oh. Lori hadn't realized Katie's condition was a direct result of the mystery—controversy—surrounding Debbie's supposed death.

And now they got a replay of all the stress. "Has she been all right? This time around, I mean?"

Ray heaved a shuddering sigh. "So far. But it was the accumulation of stress that did it last time, I think. And the not knowing."

Lori supposed that at least they could know for sure now what had happened to their daughter. But that came with baggage of its own. Like, *where had she been* and *why didn't she tell us she wasn't dead all these years?*

She honestly couldn't say which would be easier to bear. But it hardly seemed fair that some of the nicest people in town had to bear both.

Ray's shoulders shook, and she realized he was crying. Lori gave his wrist a squeeze. "I'm so sorry," she said, her voice as gentle as an ocean breeze at sunset.

"It's not that—it is, it is, but it isn't." He took a deep breath and wiped his face. "I've lost my daughter twice, and now—I'll lose Katie too."

"She'll be okay. It's hard, I know, but—"

"Debbie disappearing almost killed Katie. What will returning from the dead do to her? To know that we weren't good enough for her, that all our worrying and heartache over the last ten years meant nothing to her, to know that she could have made it all better at any second if she'd just picked up the phone, but *she didn't want to.*" He jerked his wrist free of Lori's hand and slammed his fist down on the tabletop over and over again.

She'd never seen Ray truly angry before today. She barely recognized him. Normally, Ray would never hurt a fly. Right now, Lori was pretty glad she wasn't an airborne insect.

Anger was a natural part of the grieving process, and she didn't begrudge him that. Violence, on the other hand, wasn't.

What had Katie said before Lori left her? Ray was liable to act out?

Had he done something when Debbie went missing to make Katie say that? Or was she kidding?

Ray shook out his hand. Somehow, he seemed even more weathered and old than normal now, even though he'd just shown off the fact that he still had his strength.

"Why weren't we enough for her?" His whisper was little more than a plaintive exhale. "Why wasn't our love enough?"

Ray broke down in tears. Lori stood to rub a hand on his back, doing what little she could to try to soothe him.

Some wounds only time could heal.

And some wounds time couldn't.

Ray sniffled loudly, wiping his face again, pulling himself together. Not for her sake, Lori hoped. "When she—the last time—" He paused to gulp air. "I was so angry. I just couldn't understand how a person could just up and disappear like that.

"So I confronted Mitch. Went to his house, late at night, practically banged down the door." Ray shook his head at his foolishness, as if this had been a youthful misjudgment. "I told him he had to tell me. I might have even punched him."

Lori was grateful she stood behind him, sparing him the shock she couldn't hide. She couldn't imagine Ray and Mitch ever not getting along.

"And that was before Katie got sick." The last word was squeezed out around the edges of emotion, and Ray wiped his face again.

"I would do anything for my Katie. Anything. And I'm just going to lose her all over again because of this."

Ray slid back into silent sobs, and Lori resumed rubbing his back as if she were comforting one of her boys as a sick child.

And as if Ray hadn't acted out the last time his daughter was in danger.

Chapter 6

Once she'd gotten Ray and Katie both calm and settled, and sat and talked with them about other things as long as they wanted, Lori headed back across the street to the inn. She checked on Shawn—no answer at his door—and the Besases—same.

Leaving her plenty of time to investigate.

Lori went to her office to write down what she'd learned from talking to Katie and Ray. The list wasn't extensive, and after she'd finished, she still felt unsettled, like the list was incomplete.

The last things Ray had said to her in the kitchen still rang in her mind. She added to her list:

- *The stress of Debbie's disappearance triggered Katie's illness.*
- *Ray worries Debbie's death might make Katie worse, even kill her.*
- *Ray would do anything to help Katie. Anything to protect her?*

The unease settled in the pit of her stomach like a giant lemon, puckering everything inside of her. Ray was willing to do anything to protect Katie. Did that include confronting the daughter who'd nearly killed her when Debbie came back to finish the job?

Lori didn't like that idea one bit. But she'd also watched Ray pound the table and heard him confess to possibly hitting Mitch. She couldn't pretend there wasn't a violent bone in his body when she knew there was.

Was Ray capable of hurting his daughter to protect his wife?

Lori definitely couldn't rule it out. And that didn't make her very happy at all.

Well, then she'd have to find another avenue for investigation.

Lori stared at the yellow legal pad. Obviously Mitch was a suspect. Obviously she should write that down. Obviously he didn't do it. Her own anger had burnt out, leaving only the hurt—but even that wasn't really his fault, wasn't something he'd done on purpose. She'd have to keep looking. She wasn't really sure which way to turn next. Her house was clean enough that she didn't really have that distraction, and she'd talked to the people who were closest to the case at the time.

Well, she hadn't exactly talked to Mitch. Or made eye contact with him. But she'd talked to Ray and Katie. The only other person who might be able to help would probably be Chip.

Chief Branson.

Probably the person least likely to help Lori's investigation in the history of Dusky Cove.

She didn't need a full rundown of his rivalry with Mitch, how much worse it had gotten when Mitch married the girl Chip loved, and how it had soured even further when, Chip assumed, Mitch murdered her.

As far as Lori knew, Chip had never married. She'd heard whispers that he still carried a torch for Debbie, and she'd seen how Chip treated Mitch whenever there was an opportunity to put him down. Mitch had never escaped the cloud of suspicion in the chief's mind.

On the other hand, it was a miracle he'd gotten out from under it in the rest of the town's.

But she'd never spoken to Chip about it. Maybe she was misinterpreting things. Reading too much into his actions.

Or maybe Chip was so mad that the woman he loved had chosen another man and then run away from him without giving him a second look. After all, he was there, still waiting for her to change her mind, loving her from afar.

Lori tossed the legal pad onto her desk. Now she'd gone a little too far, imputing motives to real people who might not actually feel that way. That didn't quite seem appropriate, especially for the chief of police.

Then again, wouldn't that be the perfect cover identity? No one would suspect the chief.

Lori shook her head at herself. She sounded like a soap opera, even in her head.

But that soap opera did have a point. What if Chip had seen Debra first and lost his temper?

No. That didn't sound like the chief. He could hold a grudge for thirty years, blame Mitch for every crime, nearly ruin his life . . . Well, maybe Chip was capable of a crime of passion.

The easiest, most direct way to resolve these questions would be to talk to Mitch himself. As hard as that sounded given what they'd just learned, she wanted to be there for him. After a quick Internet search, Lori found the phone number for the county jail. She listened to the menu options and pressed the right numbers to get to the visitors' hotline. Finally she got ahold of an actual person. "I'm calling to arrange a visit to Mitch Griffin," Lori said.

"All right, let me see." The line was silent for a moment. "Um, it says here he's not taking visitors."

"No, that can't be right. Is he not *allowed* visitors?" Could the county be just as biased against Mitch as Chief Branson?

"Um." The operator paused again. "It looks like he has declined all visitors."

"Even Lori Keyes?"

"I don't have any exceptions listed."

Lori sank back in her chair. Mitch didn't want to see her? That couldn't mean . . .

No. "Thanks," Lori murmured before she hung up.

All right, then. The second easiest, most direct way to resolve these questions would be to talk to Chip himself. Which he probably wouldn't like. Especially not once she started poking directly at his alibi.

At least once, her interviews had gotten her in trouble. There had been that one girl in particular who threw a whole glass of iced tea at Lori for asking about her alibi.

Lori had known Chip for two years. Granted, they'd never been close enough to be friends, but in the last twenty-four hours, he'd been a different person from the one she'd known.

He'd punched Mitch. He'd wept over Debbie's body. He'd intimidated her.

She'd obviously known he was the jealous type already. You had to be to hold it against a guy when a woman chooses you over him and grasp that grudge like a lifeline even after you thought she was dead.

Until you found out she wasn't, and your whole world turned upside down. Innocent exterior. What was lurking on the inside?

Lori gathered her courage and drove the short distance to the police station. Inside and out, it wasn't hard to tell that it was a converted house. The stucco exterior did little to hide the shape of the original home—especially with the cozy porch and rocking chairs out front. Unless the police needed a kindler, gentler image—unlikely in a town small enough where the police force was related to half of it—it showed how laidback the town and its law enforcement normally was.

Or was before Lori had moved here.

Lori marched right up to Doris, the nonagenarian dispatcher, and laid her hands on the desk. "I need to speak with the chief," Lori announced.

"He's in a meeting," Doris said. "Feel free to wait."

Lori settled, wishing she enjoyed a handicraft like knitting or crochet or even needlepoint, but she wasn't coordinated enough for that kind of thing. Plus, when she'd tried, she'd always managed to lose all her accouterments and that was the end of her handy traveling hobby.

Still, it would have been nice to have something to keep her mind off the waiting and the persistent nagging of what she was about to do.

Lori glanced around the police station. Inside, the floor plan still resembled a residence. The living room was now a reception area, the kitchen a break room, and the bedrooms offices. She didn't even think they'd changed the carpet when they'd converted it. As far as Lori knew, they didn't even have a holding cell here in town. When they'd arrested her two years ago, she'd gone straight to the county jail.

A memory she'd rather erase.

How had she not known all these years that Mitch had been through the same thing?

And it was very likely he was going through it again. She pushed aside a pang at the thought of him all alone there. Was that what he wanted?

At least the chief hadn't suspected Lori herself of Debbie's murder. She made a decent suspect, really. Why wouldn't the new girlfriend want the old wife out of the way?

But, then, there could have only been one suspect in the chief's mind.

A door in the back opened, and Lori hopped to her feet. The chief strode out of the back hallway, followed by someone who seemed vaguely familiar. Lori thought she remembered him from the crime scene the night before.

"Thanks, Edelblute," the chief murmured, shaking his hand before the other man left.

The chief didn't seem to notice Lori, but he definitely could have been ignoring her. Wouldn't have been the first time.

"Chip?" Lori tried. Better to appeal to his humanity than his office, maybe?

He glanced at her, but turned back to Doris, pointing out something in the papers on the desk. In addition to working dispatch, Doris was their secretary, office manager and pretty much mother.

The chief finished with his instructions and turned for his office again.

"Chief," Lori said, in a tone that she hoped sounded like she knew he wouldn't dare to ignore something so urgent.

His shoulders dropped, and he turned back to her. "What do

you want?" His voice said he already knew and didn't want to hear.

But she was going to say it anyway. "I want to talk. About Debbie."

The word seemed to wound him, and he winced. "We've got a handle on it, Lori."

Although his tone wasn't harsh, Lori wasn't going to stand for that. "Do you want justice for her? Or do you just want to punish Mitch?"

"Can't I have both?" Chip cracked a smile. He looked younger than her with that face. At Lori's stern expression, he quickly sobered.

Good to know she hadn't lost her motherly touch.

"Listen, Lori," he said, trying that gentle tone again, "I don't want to be doing this. I wish none of this had happened." His voice fell to a murmur. "You have no idea how much I want that to be true."

"I know. I really do."

Chip nodded, acknowledging that this wasn't easy for her either, watching someone she loved suffering. Or, not watching right now. "You find a better suspect, you tell me," Chip said. "But right now the guy I've got behind bars is the one who's spent the last ten years thinking his wife was dead, with the rest of the town saying he'd killed her. How mad do you think he'd be to find her alive? What do you think he'd be capable of in that situation?"

"Not this. Nobody in town thinks he killed her anymore."

The chief arched an eyebrow, and Lori realized that maybe she didn't know the gossip quite as well as she thought. Would her friends—especially the town's reigning gossip queen, Kim Yates—keep her in the dark? Because she was dating Mitch?

But wouldn't that be all the more reason to warn someone you cared about?

Lori mentally added *get a neutral opinion about Mitch's innocence* to her to-do list and turned back to the matter at hand. "What if you've spent so long thinking he's guilty that you can't see him any other way?"

She braced herself at the backlash that would inevitably follow. The chief wasn't exactly a fan of her correcting him, and it had happened a lot more often than either of them liked.

"When Debbie went missing ten years ago, who reported her?"

"Oh, that was Kim Yates," Doris piped up. Lori turned to her—maybe the old woman was the person she should have been interviewing all along. "She missed their weekly girl's night at the nail parlor."

Lori nodded in a go-on gesture. "Mitch wasn't the one to report her?"

"No, he claimed he was out working and hadn't seen that she was gone. Said he figured she'd gone straight to the salon with Kim."

"Did that seem unusual?"

"No, Lori," Chip broke in. "It was totally normal. That was why we arrested him. For doing absolutely nothing suspicious."

"Well, what did he do that made him look suspicious, then?" Lori didn't mean for her tone to sound confrontational, but it did come out that way.

Chip ticked off the reasons on his thick fingers. "One, he sold the boat that he'd allegedly taken her out on the water with about three days later. Two, he didn't want us to search his house for evidence. We can't hold that against him by law, but this is Dusky Cove. He shouldn't have had anything to hide."

Lori was far from a legal expert, but she was fairly certain that selling a boat and refusing a warrantless search didn't exactly meet the standard of probable cause.

"And," the chief added, acting almost like it pained him to lay this evidence on top of the already preponderous pile, "there's the little fact that she must have broken his heart."

Those words snagged along the thoughts flowing through Lori's mind as she'd waited for Chip. "Didn't she break yours, too?"

Chip quirked both eyebrows this time. "I'm sorry?"

Lori realized she only knew Mitch's side of the story when it came to his rivalry with Chip. Maybe he didn't think of it the same way. "Did she pick Mitch over you?"

Chip snorted. "In high school. It's been thirty years."

"Right. But if she didn't want to be with Mitch anymore—ten years ago—why didn't she divorce him and marry you?"

The chief stared at her, his neck growing pink above his collar. "You don't know what you're talking about."

"You're right; I don't. But I know I'd be upset if the person I'd carried a torch for for thirty years suddenly turned up to tell me there'd never been anything between us. That she'd rather play dead than be with me."

Now the chief was flat-out mad. "Lori, don't pretend like you knew Debra, or me, or the situation ten years ago."

"I'm trying to understand that. Don't you think that's got *something* to do with why she showed up again—dead?"

The red spread up into his cheeks. "You don't know what you're talking about. You don't know anything about my history with Debra."

"I'd love to hear more about it. When did you date? How did it end? Why did she choose Mitch?" As soon as the name crossed her lips, Lori bit them, as if she could bite back the words she'd just said. That was a mistake.

Chip took two steps toward her, looming over her like a menacing threat. Lori's heart shrank, and she cast a glance at Doris. The chief followed her line of sight before finally backing off a step. "For the last time. You don't know anything about the situation. For once in your life, keep your nose out of our business."

The words carried a vehemence belied by their very normal volume. Lori just nodded slowly. "Okay."

To be honest, it wasn't his words or his tone that had her cowed; it was the way he'd just purposefully tried to intimidate her. Or worse. What would he have done if Doris hadn't been there?

Lori looked over at the old woman behind the desk, fixated on them with rapt attention. Lori turned to go, still so taken aback by the chief's threat that she almost didn't know which way was out.

"Here," the chief said, and Lori thought he was going to show her out. Instead, he grabbed a paper off Doris's desk and shoved it into Lori's hands.

Lori stared down at the 1980s Glamour Shot of a woman with dark hair. *In loving memory*, the caption read. *Debra E W Griffin, 1959-2002*

"Never forget there is a real victim here." Somehow, his words seemed to carry even more of a threat.

"Sorry." Lori half-stumbled to the street, still trying to calm her racing heart.

She'd never seen Chip behave that way before, and she'd stuck her nose pretty far into police business more than once. The case was obviously more personal to him—to both of them.

Lori hurried to her car and got in, locking her doors behind her. She glanced back at the door, past the porch with the rockers. What would have happened if it weren't for Doris, Lori wondered again. The chief wouldn't have hurt her.

Would he?

And if he was mad at Lori for trying to talk about Debra—all right, and for provoking him, she wasn't totally innocent of that—but if merely talking about Debra made the chief that mad, how would he react to seeing her after all this time?

Obviously, the chief had thought she'd been dead for the last ten years instead of living heaven knows where, pretending her life in Dusky Cove had never happened—including Mitch.

And Chip.

What would he do if the love of his life—who he really did still love, somehow—showed up and rubbed it in his face that she didn't want him?

How angry would that make him?

Lori had just seen him resort to violence last night. He'd hit Mitch without even a moment's hesitation, no split-second consideration of the badge he wore. What if that wasn't the first time?

She stared at the beige stucco of the police station for a long time, as if she could read the minds of its occupants.

The stucco had no answers.

And neither did Lori.

But every time she talked to someone else, she certainly came up with a lot more questions.

Chapter 7

ori only made it as far as her parlor before her investigation was interrupted again by her guests.

Or, rather, her guests reminded her that innkeeping was her real job.

"Hello!" Manuel Besas called, strolling in after her. "The beach was wonderful."

"Nothing like relaxing in the waves," Chelsea sighed. "Thank you for the picnic basket!" She handed over the wicker basket.

"You're so welcome," Lori said, returning their broad smiles. Her mind, however, was running through ways to get rid of them so she could go back to hunting for the truth.

"We're going to go clean up for dinner," Chelsea announced, faster than if she'd been reading Lori's mind.

Of course, if she'd read Lori's mind—or the flyer still in Lori's hand—she probably wouldn't have been smiling anymore. "Sounds great."

Lori was alone in her office before the Besases even made it halfway up the stairs. She set Debra's flyer down next to her computer. No matter who she'd hurt in her life, Debra was the victim. She deserved justice too.

Finally recovered from her brush with Chief Branson, Lori's mind had latched onto an important little fact: Doris has said it was Kim who reported Debra missing. Lori shot off a quick text to ask Kim to come over, then warmed up some breakfast leftovers from the freezer. That had become her safe place when it came to food—but she could only poke at them.

How did the most important men in her life—other than her sons, of course—suddenly become potential murderers? Mitch, Ray, even Chip. She didn't want to believe it of any of them, but she also couldn't dismiss them either. She'd let herself overlook people she cared about in the past, and that almost ended very badly for them all.

Lori was washing her plate when the knock came at the back door. Few people came to this door, so Lori could guess who it might be.

The stupid hope bloomed in her chest against her will, but that hope died when she looked out the window and saw Kim standing there. Kim offered her a small smile and a wave, and Lori opened the door for her.

Of course it wasn't Mitch. He was in jail.

Kim gave her a quick squeeze. "How are you holding up?"

"Trying to keep busy." But keeping busy by investigating the very thing that upset her wasn't exactly a recipe for happiness.

This was a murder investigation. By definition there was no "happiness."

"Anything I can do to help you with that?" Kim asked.

"I need to work while I think. And talk. Is that okay?"

"Of course."

Lori crossed the kitchen to where she'd hung up an idea list. She couldn't bear to do a formal menu plan—she'd only end up changing it at the last minute anyway—but a list of ideas gave her the freedom to pick what sounded good now. "I'd like to prep for breakfast tomorrow. I saw this interesting breakfast sausage on the Internet." She pulled down the three-ring binder that held the printouts of her ideas and thumbed through until she found the right recipe.

"Cherry tarragon?" Kim murmured. She looked to Lori. "You'll have to let me know how these taste."

If that was Kim declining to help, she'd have to be more direct. Lori directed her. "There's a package of ground pork in the fridge. Will you grab it?"

Kim turned to obey, and Lori headed for the pantry to gather the spices, an onion, and a bag of dried cherries. Kim put the dried cherries in water and measured the spices while Lori plopped the ground pork into a bowl and then chopped onions.

"Have you been investigating?" Kim asked. The tone of her voice said she already knew the answer. How could Lori not?

Just like Kim couldn't keep away from teasing out gossip, Lori couldn't keep away from teasing out the truth when it came to a murder investigation. It wasn't a question of whether she wanted to or not. It was a question of getting to the bottom of it.

"I've spoken to Ray and to Chip, but I still don't have a good handle on what happened when Debra went missing ten years ago."

"I'm afraid the only person who knows what really happened won't be able to tell us anymore."

It wasn't like Kim not to offer speculation or some small smidgen of dirt—and this had to have been the most scandalous thing to hit the town in half a century. Hadn't Doris said Kim reported Debra missing?

"I heard you knew more about it at the time," Lori said, walking a fine line with her words.

Kim nodded slowly. "A little."

"You reported her missing."

"Well, she was. She missed our appointment. I've never had a friend like her again." She dropped her measuring spoon and turned to Lori. "No offense."

"None taken." Lori took the little bowl where Kim had poured the spices and dumped it into the bowl with the pork. "What did you think happened at the time?"

"At first, I was worried she'd been in an accident, of course, and then the longer it went that day, the more I wondered. When I found out there wasn't an accident, that nobody had seen her since she went out with Mitch—" Kim broke off.

"You've known Mitch a long time, too."

"Of course."

"And sometimes knowing someone a long time—and being

friends with their spouse—means you get to know another side of them, don't you?"

She wasn't even being subtle about fishing for information, but Lori didn't care even a little bit. This was information she was practically entitled to.

Lori gave Kim a minute to gather her thoughts while she mixed the sausage ingredients. By the time they were well combined, Kim was waiting for Lori to meet her eyes.

"Help me shape the patties?" Lori asked.

"Of course." Kim scooped out the perfect amount of sausage filling and shaped it into a palm-sized coin. The task seemed to give her something to focus on other than the words she needed to say. "I don't want you to take this the wrong way, but Mitch and Debbie were having a tough time at the end."

"In their marriage?"

Kim nodded, patting the edges of her second patty. "I tried not to think less of Mitch, but when your best friend only tells you the bad things in their relationship, you tend to worry. Still, I don't really think everything was his fault. Debbie was . . . she wasn't herself for a while at the end. And when we'd talk, she really seemed to focus on him, when I really thought she needed help. Professional help."

Lori assumed she didn't mean a maid. She placed another patty on the sheet pan. She'd have to clear off a shelf in the fridge to make room for this, but it would be worth it tomorrow. "What kind of behavior are you talking about?"

"Well." Kim scooped up the meat for another patty. "She seemed . . . sad. Dark. She talked a lot about how unhappy she was—how she felt like she was screaming on the inside. Sometimes, she said that the only thing that had helped was going on vacation. Maybe that was what she ended up doing, taking ten years' vacation from her life." Kim sighed at her own joke. "She just felt like she was under pressure all the time."

"From Mitch?" Lori found that hard to believe. If anything, Mitch had been supportive and encouraging of Lori, whether it was sound marketing plans or a harebrained scheme to catch a killer.

"I don't know." Kim paused, lost in memory for a moment. "More like she actually, physically felt the pressure. She was stressed. Burned out. Done. And Mitch didn't want a divorce. He wanted to fight for their marriage."

"Was it too late?"

"Who can make that call?" Kim set down her latest sausage patty and turned to Lori. "I think they could have turned it around, but only if Debbie could get her head right. She was in denial of how serious her problem was."

"So it didn't surprise you to find out she really had run away from everything here?"

Kim snorted. "Of course it surprised me that my best friend faked her own death successfully for ten years and then showed up dead."

Lori heard the way Kim's voice caught on best friend. But for the first time, someone she was interviewing wasn't revealing their own violent tendencies and deep-seated anger, just pain. For the friend she'd lost, for the reasons she might never understand.

"Where do you think she's been for the last ten years?"

"Wilmington? Walla Walla, Washington?" Kim chuckled to herself. "She could have been anywhere. Anywhere but here."

Lori tried to put herself in that mindset, but the only thing she'd ever wanted to run away from was grief, and that followed you. She couldn't imagine being so unhappy that you sacrificed every relationship you had for a chance to start over.

Lori placed the last sausage patty on the tray, and she and Kim washed their hands again. Lori covered the tray and stuck it in the fridge to leave them to fry in the morning. Without evening meal prep, she'd never be able to put on the big breakfasts her guests had come to love.

Kim turned to Lori, her eyes serious. "After everything shook out last time, Mitch gave me Debbie's journal. He said he couldn't bear to read it. He probably should have."

Lori quirked an eyebrow.

"She was a lot unhappier than any of us knew. I mean, if you knew her, it wasn't like you could miss it. This light inside her had just gone out for some reason. But the stuff in the journal." Kim shook her head. "I hadn't realized her relationship with Mitch had deteriorated that badly, if the journal is to be believed."

Lori found herself clutching the edge of the stainless steel countertop. "Was he hurting her?"

Kim took a deep breath, buying time before she answered. When she finally did, she obviously chose her words carefully. "Not on purpose."

Lori frowned. "Do many people know this?"

"No. This is the first time I've told anyone."

Lori snapped to look at her. The gossip queen hadn't talked about the biggest, juiciest story to hit their shores in five decades?

"I know, I know. It's just—this time, I really knew it wasn't my right. Debbie wasn't coming from a good place at the time, and I didn't know if the stuff in the journal reflected more that than anything Mitch did or didn't do. But I could never be sure."

"Did *you* think Mitch killed her?"

Kim sighed and leaned against the edge of the counter. "For the first couple weeks, I was a hundred percent sure she was coming back. Even when he sold the boat—he said he'd already negotiated that deal and it was only the pickup we'd seen. And then weeks and months passed, and I couldn't help but wonder."

"Whether Mitch did it?"

"How—*why* he would have done it. He was the one who wanted to fight for the marriage. By the time she started talking to him, according to the journal at least, she'd already felt like there was nothing to be done for them. For her life."

Lori still couldn't picture feeling that way, but her heart ached for Debbie just the same. "Did she sound suicidal?"

Kim studied her hands. "That was what I thought happened, right up until yesterday."

"What do you think now?"

Kim's sigh was deep and wide-ranging and sad. "I don't think we'll ever know anymore. It just breaks my heart that it happened this way. It's so much more . . . real this time around. I guess having the body to bury does that."

"Did they have a funeral?"

"Yeah, after about six weeks, her parents finally accepted that she wasn't coming home, so we had services for her. Probably the saddest funeral that church has ever seen."

Lori couldn't even imagine what that would be like. Giving up on ever seeing your daughter again. Not knowing what had happened. Not even being sure she was dead. How did you handle that kind of loss and come out still liking the person everyone else seemed to blame?

"Did the town think Mitch did it?"

Kim pressed her lips together, twisting them to the side. "Let's just say there was some nudging away from that."

Lori read between the lines: Kim had put her prodigious skills at cultivating the town's gossip mill to good use—and actual good, this time. "You didn't tell people she'd committed suicide, did you?"

Kim shook her head quickly. "None of my business if she did, and that was just speculation."

That hadn't often stopped Kim before, but Lori buttoned her mouth.

"I was just very good at pointing out that there was no evidence, physical or circumstantial, that even proved she was dead. *Habeas corpus* and all that." She threw around the Latin phrase like an old court hand.

"Do you still have her journal?"

Kim's gaze fell to the tile floor. "It was too personal. I gave it back to Mitch."

Lori nodded slowly. "Did you ever let Ray and Katie see it?"

"Oh, no, no, no. They had a hard enough time as it was. I mean, I was friends with Mitch, too, so the things she said about him in the diary, I could see his side too. But her parents? They'd never see him the same way, and they needed each other's strength to get through this."

Lori remembered Ray's hinting at violence the first time around.

Why was everyone hitting Mitch? Why was he just taking it? Wouldn't an innocent person stand up for themselves?

But now they could all see he was innocent of the first "murder." What did that mean for the second?

Kim's eyes rested on Lori, full of compassion. "I know this isn't easy for you. Nobody says you have to look into this one."

Lori decided not to argue with her, studying the scratches on her countertop.

"Even if I did have the journal," Kim continued, "I don't think I'd want to turn it over. It's just too prejudicial."

Again with the legal terminology. Lori hadn't seen this side of her friend before—or the side that protected someone's privacy. "Why do you say that?"

"Like I said, if you didn't know Mitch, if you'd never heard his side of the story, you would think less of him."

"I thought you said it didn't make him look guilty."

"I said it didn't make me think murder. But the way she talked about needing to escape her life, feeling like the walls were closing in, and all the while, Mitch refused to listen or even argued with her . . ." Kim grabbed a rag and swiped at an invisible spot on the counter. "He couldn't see what she was saying, and she probably wasn't telling him in a way he could understand. He wanted to stay near her parents—they've been like parents to him for the last twenty-some years—close to everything they'd always had, close to the life they'd built. She felt like that life was suffocating her."

"You saw all this happening from the outside, right?"

Kim shrugged.

"Is that a yes or a no?"

"She didn't tell me everything. But she talked a little about this. After she was gone, that was when I got Mitch's perspective."

"And what did you think? Was her life unbearable?"

"I thought she was unhappy, but there wasn't a *reason*. There doesn't have to be a reason to be depressed."

Lori almost startled. "You think she was depressed?"

"Her journal makes it sound that way. And I don't think anyone in their right mind could kill themselves."

Perhaps not. Lori rolled the information around in her mind. All that evidence probably would have made her think Mitch did it, if she only had the diary, or that Debbie had committed suicide.

But now they knew neither were true.

"So it looks like she . . . ran away instead?"

Kim looked away, and Lori caught a glimpse of the tears glistening in her eyes. "I guess so. I just wish . . . I would have helped her, you know? I mean, I'm not a psychologist or anything, but if I'd really understood what she was feeling, I would have done anything to get her help."

In that moment, Lori realized just how hard this must be for Kim—who'd been there to comfort Lori all along. Kim had lost her best friend and for nearly a decade assumed that she'd killed herself. Now, she'd discovered that the friend she loved and wanted to help had rejected Kim along with her own parents and husband and everyone else she'd ever known.

And for what?

Unlike every other person she'd actually talked to about Debbie, though, Kim wasn't angry. She was just sad—for what might have been, what she might have been able to do, how she'd failed.

The creak of the middle stair carried through the kitchen wall, and Lori and Kim both turned toward the sound. "Looks like my guests are ready for dinner."

Kim patted her shoulder. "I'll let you get to work. Let me know if I can help with anything else."

Lori thanked her and let her out the back door before heading to the parlor to intercept her guests if they hadn't already left.

Instead of the Besases, however, Lori found Shawn in the parlor, bleary-eyed as if he'd just overslept both lunch and dinner. Maybe sleep was the only vacation he could get from losing his wife.

"Feeling any better?" Lori asked, though her tone betrayed her—obviously he wasn't.

Shawn rubbed his eyes. "Do you have any recommendations for dinner?"

"My standby is Brunswick stew at the Salty Dog, with hush puppies, of course." Half a second too late, Lori remembered she should throw some business Kim's way as a thank you. "The Mimosa Café has some great soups and salads, too."

He nodded absently, as if he wasn't listening at all.

"Would you like me to order something for you?"

Shawn looked at her, as if he'd just remembered she was there. "Uh, no, no, I can get it myself. Thanks, though."

Lori let him out the front, making sure he had his keys, and locked the door behind him. But no sooner had she closed it than the Besases came downstairs, still looking like they'd absorbed the sun's brightness. Such a contrast from Shawn. They headed out to eat, but before Lori could close the door, a tall, broad-shouldered man stepped onto her porch. He looked to be about her age, maybe a couple years older. "Do you have any vacancies?" he asked.

"I do," Lori said. She quoted the man her rates, but he was already nodding before she even finished.

"I'll take it," he said, pulling out his wallet. "Two nights."

"Wonderful." Lori read his credit card: Jared Lehanneur.

Where had she heard that name before? "Oh," she exclaimed once she'd placed it. "Do you have family in the area?"

"I used to," Jared admitted. "Hey, do the Watsons still own the shop across the street?"

"Yes, they do."

His smile held something Lori couldn't quite put her finger on, but whatever it was, it didn't quite sit well with her. She should refuse the booking, really—she was no fool, though she'd never had occasion to exercise that right before—but her investigator sense told her Jared might know something helpful. "Let me grab a form to get your info," Lori said. "I'll be right back."

"I'll be here." Jared grinned again.

Again, a chill swept over Lori's scalp.

Chapter 8

The next morning, the cherry tarragon sausages were a hit with the Besases, and Jared seemed pleased. It was hard to tell whether he meant his compliments or was mocking her with the sinister bent to his smile, though.

But even Shawn managed to choke a couple patties down, so that had to mean something.

The Besases headed off to explore historic downtown, Shawn was bound for the Salt Marsh Boardwalk, and Jared was going to . . . church? Lori tried not to act surprised, though it wasn't all that often her guests—vacationers—headed off to visit a congregation and a pastor they'd never met before. But Lori just smiled and bid her guest goodbye.

Once she had the breakfast dishes in the sink and linens in the laundry, Lori changed into her favorite fluttery yellow skirt and headed to church herself. She wasn't entirely sure it was wise for her to attend church either after all that had happened the last few days, but if anyone needed comfort now, it was her.

Unfortunately, she didn't find it. Pastor Bill walked to the pulpit and began his sermon with some thoughts on Palm Sunday today. Lori's attention wandered a bit until Pastor Bill suddenly captured it again with a scripture: "'For I was hungry and you gave Me food; I was thirsty and you gave Me drink; I was a stranger and you took Me in; I was naked and you clothed Me; I was sick and you visited Me; I was in prison and you came to Me.'"

Lori flinched inwardly. This was why she'd felt out of sorts. Yes, she wasn't making progress with the case, and obviously she couldn't discount the emotional impact the turmoil of the last two days had on her. But in the end, she'd abandoned Mitch when he needed her.

He deserved for her to at least try to talk to him about what happened.

She knew how awful it was to sit in that jail all weekend, your humanity eroding away as you sit alone, behind bars, even the basic dignity of using the bathroom taken from you.

If he wasn't going to see her, she was just going to have to insist.

She stood up, edged past Lillian Hunter and Tina Mendez, and headed straight for the car.

The drive to the county jail was only about half an hour, but that was plenty of time to contemplate what she might say to Mitch when she saw him.

It wasn't enough time, however, to decide whether that first sentence should be "I'm sorry I haven't been here" or "What on earth happened?"

Lori filled out the forms and settled in a hard, plastic chair in the waiting area. A comfortable guest parlor this was not. They may be criminals behind the bars—Mitch wasn't one, was he?—but did their guests have to be punished too?

After what felt like an eternity on that hard chair, Lori stood up. What could be taking so long? He wouldn't really turn her away if she was already here, would he?

Of course not.

Surely it didn't take this long to go and get him. Her own stint in jail was short enough that she hadn't really had a chance to get visitors—and the only person who would have visited was the one who'd put her there. Mitch would want her to visit, would want her support. Right?

Unless he did this, and he was taking the punishment just as he'd absorbed Chip's punch two nights ago.

Lori realized she was pacing and plopped down in the hard,

plastic chair again. The jolt racked through her bones.

After a few more minutes, and a few more rounds of pacing the room, the door to the waiting area swung open and a uniformed guard stepped in. He looked vaguely familiar—had Lori met him when she was a prisoner? Did the women's wing use the same guards as the men's?

"Um, Miss Keyes?"

"Yes?"

"I'm sorry, but the prisoner doesn't want visitors right now."

For a moment, defeat smothered her thoughts.

But she wouldn't give in. She'd just have to convince Mitch—and this guard—to let her see him anyway. "Excuse me?" Her tone of voice very clearly turned to that of a mother reprimanding a child.

The corrections officer stepped back a bit, his face showing chagrin. But it wasn't him she was trying to reprimand. She crossed the room toward the guard, trying to figure out whether she should bully or plead with him.

Pleading would probably come off better for her. The man doubtlessly dealt with enough bullying on a daily basis that she couldn't hope to do a better job than the people in this prison. "Officer, please. He's been through something terrible—I was with him when he found the body—but I really don't think he did it. I can't be sure, though, unless I get a chance to talk to him. Is there any way you can get him out here?"

The guard frowned. "I'm afraid it's his choice, ma'am."

"Well, how long until he gets bail then?" When Lori had been arrested, late on a Friday, she'd had to spend the full weekend in jail until a judge set her bail and she could leave. She imagined it would be the same for Mitch.

"His bail will be set tomorrow, but I wouldn't hold out hope. The judge might not give him bail, and if he does, it's going to be high."

"Familiar with the case?" Lori asked.

He nodded. "My wife went to high school with Debbie."

Lori winced. "And Mitch, then, too."

"Yeah."

The undercurrent in his voice was unmistakable. "You don't think it looks good for Mitch?"

"I don't know, just what I've heard around here, but seems like most of the jail has already made up its mind about him. Probably did years ago."

"So did Chief Branson," Lori pointed out. Hopefully if this guard knew Debbie, he'd know of Chip and Mitch and their rivalry—and how this could very well be the antithesis of justice.

"Listen, I know he's not taking visitors. But—please—I'm worried about him. I need to see him. Can you let him know?"

She hadn't planned to say that, but the words just tumbled out of her. When she heard her own voice echoing back to her, the words struck Lori to the heart. Because they were true. Maybe she didn't know what to think about Mitch and what he had or hadn't done, but she was worried about him. She did care. She did need to see him.

The officer nodded slowly. "I'll try to convince him. Again."

"Thank you." Lori mustered a small smile, then fell back into pacing once the door closed behind the corrections officer again.

Immediately, she also set to worrying. What if he didn't want to see her? What would she do then? What would that mean? That he'd done it? He was guilty and didn't want her help, didn't want her to waste her time? Or that he just *felt* guilty, like he probably had for the last ten years, like he might forever?

Of course, it was entirely possible that he didn't want to see her because he didn't want to face his inadvertent attempt at bigamy.

Lori realized the sharp staccato tapping of her heels across the floor meant she was more marching than pacing, trying to burn off that frustrated energy. Without much success in this cramped little cage, unfortunately.

The wait gave her a chance to revise her half-formed plans, though. Now, she was certain that the first thing she'd say to him was, "What were you thinking?"

It was a good thing this room was security-proofed, because

she might have punctuated that question with a projectile if everything weren't bolted down.

At last, a knock came at the door, and the officer poked his head in again. "He's willing to talk to you."

This time, Lori was sitting down, and she hopped to her feet. "Really?"

"Wasn't easy, but I convinced him."

Lori was fairly certain he had more important things to be doing than persuading an inmate to meet with a girlfriend—or maybe ex-girlfriend—so she was doubly grateful. "Thanks for talking to him." She tried to beam at the guard to convey the depth of her gratitude, but she probably just came off looking like a deranged cartoon hyena, she was so on edge.

At least she was getting out of the waiting room. The corrections officer led Lori down a short hallway to a large room dipped in white paint. She sat at a cafeteria table, the kind with its benches connected to the tabletop, and waited.

She was so pleased to get out of the waiting room, only to end up waiting here instead. Although the bench was a little more comfortable on her hips than the hard, plastic chairs had been.

The corrections officer briefed her on the proper behavior— no touching, no arguing, no shouting, etc., etc.—before leaving her there to wait.

It seemed to take years for Mitch to finally emerge from the other doorway in the room. He was handcuffed and dressed in a faded orange jumpsuit, looking for all the world like he'd already been convicted in more than the court of public opinion.

A surge of emotion filled her chest, and Lori stood, biting back tears. "Mitch," she said, the name soft on her lips again.

He couldn't look at her but shuffled over to the table where she sat.

"Are you okay?" she asked. Not what she'd planned on leading with, but now, seeing him dressed as an inmate, it was the most pressing question.

Mitch shrugged. "Not exactly Club Med in here."

Lori managed an almost soundless laugh, settling on the

bench again. "Believe me, I know."

"I remember." Mitch sat at the table across from her, his eyes fixed on the faux wood-grain veneer. "Why did you come?"

Wasn't that obvious? Lori leaned in, a quick glance at the guard to make sure this was okay, and lowered her voice. "Listen, I've been doing some digging—"

"Why?"

She startled and stopped short. "What do you mean, 'Why'? Did you plan on going to jail for this?"

"I don't know anymore. I didn't kill her, but . . . I'm not sure I don't deserve this."

Lori pulled back. "What are you saying? What does that mean?"

Mitch's hands, large, rough, talented, the hands she'd held so many times, now rubbed at one another, his only answer.

"Did you . . . did you do this?" she barely breathed.

"No." Mitch's voice was quiet but clear. "I didn't kill Debbie. But . . ." He heaved a deep breath. "I drove her away."

Lori watched him, waiting for more of an explanation, but that was apparently all he'd offer. "What, in your car?"

Mitch finally met her eyes, and his carried sarcasm. "Yeah, right up to the bus station, where I bought her a ticket, waved goodbye, and said, 'Have a nice life, honey!'"

"Then what *do* you mean?"

"I didn't listen. She told me so many times and so many ways that she needed something to change, and I don't know if I didn't believe her or I just didn't want to change, but I let it go on too long—and then she was gone."

The pieces of this ever-shifting puzzle slid around in Lori's brain. So Mitch did know that Debbie wanted out, wanted their life to be different, and he blamed himself for not delivering that. And that was why she disappeared.

Obviously he'd read her diary and figured out what he'd done wrong. Did he draw the same conclusions that Kim had? "What did you think happened to her?" Lori asked.

Mitch looked away again, transforming back into that distant person he'd been ever since that night. Not the person she'd fallen in love with. Someone withdrawn and small and even frightened.

Someone damaged. So badly burned he had to protect himself at all costs.

Lori tried to tamp down on the instinct to help him. Helping him wouldn't get her closer to the truth, and that was something she and Mitch both needed, especially if there was to be any hope of this relationship moving forward.

Of course, unless she wanted the county jail as a wedding venue, they might not be able to do that no matter what they felt.

Yet another reason she needed the truth—and she needed it to be on Mitch's side.

But his silence suggested—screamed—that it wasn't.

"Whatever you're holding back," Lori said, "out with it. I'm not here as your girlfriend. I'm here as a citizen investigating. You keeping things from me—*again*," she couldn't help but add, emphasizing that word most of all, "is not going to help your case."

"I didn't ask for help." Mitch raised his gaze to a point over her shoulder.

"Well, to be honest, I'm not doing this for you. I'm doing this for Ray and Katie. Don't they deserve to know what really happened to their daughter?"

Mitch's focus shifted to her, but the hollow look in his eyes spoke for him before he could. "No," he said when his voice finally caught up. "They can't—I can't—they'd never forgive me."

Chills crawled down Lori's neck. But she knew Mitch hadn't killed Debbie—not ten years ago, definitely.

"Or her," Mitch added. "It would break them. Probably kill Katie. You can't."

Lori glanced at the guard, to see if he'd heard the word "kill," but he stood in faithful silence, betraying nothing. Then she focused her best, hardest stare on Mitch. The I-mean-business stare. The I'm-not-leaving-until-you-tell-me-young-man stare.

Mitch rubbed his hair, then dropped his hands to the table

again. "I knew."

"Knew. What." She made her voice as hard as her eyes.

"I knew she was alive."

Lori waited for the realization to sink in, but it didn't. Hadn't Ray basically said that?

Unless . . . unless Mitch *knew*. Not in the metaphysical way that a parent might "know" their child couldn't be dead.

In the very physical way that someone who had evidence would know that a person actually was not dead.

"How? What, did she contact you? Drain your bank accounts? Blackmail you?"

Mitch rolled his eyes with a frustrated sigh. "Everything was too perfect at home. Too tidy. All her things packed away. Like she'd planned on not coming back. It didn't feel . . . right."

"So she was still alive because she cleaned the house?" Lori didn't bother hiding her incredulity. "That's evidence?" She scoffed. "That's the type of investigation I'd expect from Chip, not you."

"She left her ring."

Lori tripped over that one for a minute. "Wasn't she going to get her nails done?"

He scrubbed his face with one massive, rough hand. "I saw her, okay? Two years after. I was in Atlanta for a botany conference, and I had to go to an ATM. I walked into the bank and . . . there she was."

"Did you talk to her?"

"At first," Mitch continued, like Lori hadn't spoken, "I tried to dismiss it. I had to be crazy. Debbie was gone. She was dead, I thought. And then I found myself standing behind her as she was filling out her deposit slip. She turned around and saw me and knew who I was."

Lori tried to picture what that would be like, but it beggared the imagination.

"She begged me not to tell her parents. I asked her if she was happy—I meant it. I'd read her journals, and I knew, I knew that I hadn't done enough for her, that I hadn't made her happy in the end. I just wanted her to be happy again." Mitch pressed both thumbs to the bridge of his nose and bowed his head, emotion choking off his words.

"Was she?" Lori asked after a moment.

"She didn't answer. She just walked away."

Atlanta was, what, six hours away? And she'd let Mitch dangle here, accused of murder, her parents writhing in the wind, for an entire decade?

Then the other pieces of the puzzle slid home. "You're telling me that you knew your wife was alive the whole time we were dating?"

Mitch sucked in a breath, then pressed his lips together. Caught.

"You were a married man pursuing a relationship with me?" Lori tried to keep her voice down, but it rose of its own accord.

"I tried not to. I tried to end it a year ago."

Lori gaped at him. "And then you took that back."

"I talked to a lawyer out in Wilmington. He said we had grounds for divorce. I just didn't know how to get in contact with her, how to do it all to keep Ray and Katie in the dark—"

"They had a right to know she was alive!"

The guard in the corner shifted, taking two steps toward the table. Lori pre-empted him, standing. "You knew she was alive all this time."

He couldn't meet her eyes. Again. Just like the night they'd found her.

The night he was going to propose.

The night he wasn't nearly as surprised as he should have been to see his wife who'd been dead for ten years.

Lori didn't have anything else to say to him. She turned and strode from the visitation room.

Chapter 9

Lori gave herself one hour. Sixty minutes to rotate the laundry, check in with her guests—all doing fine—and bawl her eyes out.

She'd fallen for a cheater. Someone who let his wife fake her own death, helped her hide from her parents who had only ever loved her—like they loved him, and he'd lied to their faces for the last eight years.

This was unbelievable.

When her mental timer was up—maybe a little closer to seventy minutes, but she'd allow it—Lori washed her face. She brushed her hair, changed into something more comfortable, washed her face again, and steeled herself for what she was about to do.

She was about to rip a family apart.

But didn't Ray and Katie deserve to know? Wasn't that the whole reason she was even investigating Debbie's death? Certainly not to stand up for that knowing, not-even-a-little-accidental philanderer.

Lori only made it to the door of her own quarters before she stopped. She needed something to soften the blow. Anything.

There was only the one answer she had for everything: food. She warmed up the four leftover cherry tarragon sausage patties and some not-exactly-homemade croissants, stuffing them in a basket with a little less care than she usually used. She was across the street before her courage could fail her again, and she let herself in their back door again.

"Ray?" she called in a low voice.

"That you, Lori?" his reply carried from upstairs.

"Yes, it's me again."

"Just a minute."

Lori set her basket on the kitchen table and fetched plates from the cabinets.

She'd call this stalling if Ray were in the room yet. So instead, it was simply preparing.

As if anything could prepare either of them for this.

And Katie . . .

She couldn't just drop this on Katie, Lori knew. She'd have to tell Ray first. He'd know what to do. Or they'd figure it out together.

Ray finally appeared on the stairs, slowly lumbering down. His eyes were bloodshot and more rheumy than usual. "How are you holding up?" he asked.

"I should be asking you that."

Ray gave her a grim frown. "We've had ten years to get used to losing Debbie. It's finding her again that's the hard part."

Guilt pierced Lori's heart. She couldn't tell him Mitch knew. Could she?

Was this simply the grown-up version of tattling? Was she doing this to get back at Mitch?

One look at the man in front of her reminded Lori that she owed it to Ray.

She pulled the chair out at the table and helped him into his seat. "Brought you some cherry tarragon sausage—homemade—and some croissants."

"Trying to fatten me up, are you?" Ray's voice was without humor.

She tried to laugh and fetched the margarine from the fridge.

"Make that butter me up." He popped open the tub and did just that with his croissant.

He needed to know. But how could she tell him? Finding out she'd been alive all this time was hard enough. Her stomach tied itself in knots in the near silence.

"Ray," Lori said slowly. He lowered his knife and croissant and looked up at her.

And she immediately lost her nerve. "Should I take a plate up to Miss Katie?"

"She'd like that." Ray turned back to his food. Was it Lori's imagination, or was he relieved?

Lori fixed the second plate and hiked the stairs to Miss Katie's room. She hoped she could buy herself some time, maybe test the waters, but Katie was asleep.

Lori headed back down to Ray.

Putting this off would only make it harder, Lori lectured herself. She needed to rip off the Band-Aid. "Ray," she said once she reached the kitchen. And again, her courage faltered. "Did you have any idea she was still alive?"

Ray whirled around so fast it practically gave Lori whiplash. "Katie? Is she okay?"

"Yes—oh, sorry. She was just asleep. I meant Debbie."

He settled back in his seat, chewing two bites of food before answering. "No parent wants their child to die first," he said at last. "I would have given anything to take her place. But at the same time . . . it just didn't feel *right* to me."

How could losing a child ever feel right?

Ray hunched over the table. "I just knew—*just knew*—she couldn't be dead. A parent always knows. We're supposed to, anyway."

Lori didn't have much firsthand experience with this, but it seemed to her that she'd seen a lot of tearful parents on the news over the years insisting that their child couldn't be dead and they felt it in their bones, swear on a stack of Bibles—and it always seemed to turn out that the child was dead.

At the same time, she believed in mother's intuition. She had to. She'd seen it work in her own life too many times to pretend it wasn't real. She wasn't a good enough parent or a smart enough person to have figured out all the times her boys needed her with the frequency that she had.

"Or," Ray said at length, "maybe you just can't kill off the hope, too. Losing your child is enough. Can't lose hope, too. So you keep hoping. Keep convincing yourself it has to be true."

Lori settled at the table with him. "Well, obviously it was true, up until yesterday."

Ray focused on his plate. "I didn't . . . I didn't think finding her would change anything."

"Of course not."

"Somewhere inside, I'd accepted it, that we probably wouldn't get to see her again. But still, that hope . . ." He turned back to his plate, cutting his sausage patty into pieces.

She'd come by before, but only Katie had been willing to talk about what had happened. Ray was only the deflated shell of the person she normally knew, but maybe that meant he was ready to really talk about what had happened. "Ray, yesterday, it kind of sounded like you did something rash when Debbie first went missing?"

He set his silverware down. "Yes. I thought Mitch had more answers. It took about two minutes to see that he was just as scared and worried as we were. We didn't understand what had happened." Ray chuckled bitterly. "You know, I even went to Chip—multiple times—just in case they were going to run off together. For a long time I thought he knew more than he was letting on, but nothing ever seemed to come of it."

Everyone, it seemed, was blindsided by Debbie's actions. Katie had suspected that Debbie was unhappy, Lori remembered from yesterday, but she didn't know if Ray had any idea about his daughter's mental state. "Did Debbie tell you she was unhappy?"

Ray nodded slowly. "We told her to find a new hobby. Forget herself and do service. Read a book."

"Did she do those things?"

"I don't know." He sighed. "She left because she was unhappy." The words were almost a question, but as if he was trying to convince himself of that fact.

"Apparently her diary said she felt trapped. One person who'd read it said she sounded depressed."

Ray looked up at that. "Depressed? Debbie?" His bushy, wild eyebrows knit together. "But she spent time with us. She could still laugh. She said she was unhappy, but . . . I didn't see it." He rubbed his forehead. "What kind of father am I? Who couldn't see his own daughter was suffering?"

"Maybe you didn't know what to look for," Lori offered. "We picture someone who's struggling like they have to be bawling and under a cloud of darkness all the time, and some of them are. But sometimes, it's more like you're just not yourself—you can't do the things you love anymore, can't be around the people you love, can't function in the way you need to. Mental illness is . . . slippery."

Ray nodded, dropping his hand. Tears dotted his cheeks. "I should have known. I should have listened better."

Maybe that was true, maybe he could have done more for his daughter, but that didn't change the past. "Blaming yourself doesn't bring her back."

He popped a bite of sausage into his mouth. "You know, even last week, I would have thought you were talking crazy talk. But—no offense, I'm sure you worked very hard on this and it's probably delicious—I can't even taste my food I'm so upset these days. The color has gone out of life. If this is how she felt all the time . . . I almost can't blame her for leaving."

Lori offered a sad smile. Mostly because of what Ray was saying, but also because of the knowledge burning inside her brain, knowing that there was someone else who deserved blame.

Could she tell Ray about this and take someone else he loved away from him?

Could she keep this secret, living across the street from him, knowing that Mitch had known all along Debbie was alive and hopefully well?

"Did you have any idea? Any inkling at all?" Lori asked. She had to admit she was stalling to put off the real question.

"I knew she couldn't be dead. Even when everyone said she had to be. I knew it." He sighed, using his fork to push the last two bites of sausage around on his plate.

"So would it surprise you to hear that someone else knew she was alive?"

Ray's head snapped up. "What do you mean? Who knew she was alive?"

"Well," Lori drew the word out, hedging. "Obviously she did, and all the people around her, wherever she was living."

He rolled his faded blue eyes, his lips tightened into a line. "You wouldn't have said that if you meant them. You mean someone I know, too. Right?"

She managed a slow nod.

"Who? Why wouldn't they tell me?"

"Would it be worse for you to not know if she was dead—when you *knew* she wasn't—or to know she was alive and wouldn't come home?"

Ray slammed a fist on the table. "Tell me who we're talking about!"

Lori met his eyes, took in the anger there. He had to already have some idea, didn't he?

His shoulders fell. "Not . . . Mitch?"

She buttoned her lips together, a non-answer that was answer enough.

Ray froze there for a very long second, just staring into space. "How could he be sure? Did she leave a note?"

"No." Lori shoved aside the feeling that she was betraying someone. She was righting a wrong. Wasn't she? "He saw her. In Atlanta."

"But how could he be sure? That he wasn't just seeing things? Do you know how many times I've thought I've seen her in the last decade?"

"He talked to her. She recognized him. Asked him not to tell."

Ray nodded as if still numb from the news. "How long?" Ray asked.

"How long . . . did he see her?"

"How long did he know she was alive?"

Lori lowered her voice. "Eight years."

The numb nod returned, bobbing his head in a rhythm that

was all instinct and conviction. Like he should have known. Like this confirmed something he'd felt deep inside.

"Are you going to tell Katie?" Lori asked

"That Debbie didn't care if she killed her mother?"

"Wait—what?"

Ray fastened a steely stare on Lori. "Losing Debbie nearly killed Katie. If I told her it all could have been avoided, it was just Debbie's choice to hurt us? What would that do to her now? What kind of stress would that put on her heart? It nearly broke the last time. It could only be worse this time."

Lori absorbed his words. She'd done something she wasn't sure about ethically or morally to tell him the truth, because they deserved to know the truth. And then Ray was doing the same the-buck-stops-here move that Mitch had pulled, keeping everyone in the dark?

There could have been reconciliation. There could have been peace. There could have been healing. Instead, there were lies and secrets and cheating.

And Ray was going to continue it all. For Katie's sake? For his own?

But did Lori have any right to stop him? Could she march upstairs and tell Katie the truth herself? She didn't want Katie's death on her hands any more than Ray did.

Lori set her jaw and let her gaze fall to the table. "No easy answers here, are there?"

"Is it bad that I almost wish she hadn't come back? That she'd stayed missing?"

Lori patted his wrist where it laid on the table. "No, I think that's pretty normal. No wrong way to grieve, you know."

Ray nodded, his gaze distant again.

Ray's words piqued a new curiosity in Lori's mind. She'd been so upset that she'd come back that Lori had never stopped to consider it: *why* had Debbie come back? She'd apparently settled and built a life in Atlanta. Had running gotten to her? The lies? Did she want closure? To say goodbye? Or did she want Mitch back? Her parents? Had she decided to reconcile with them all?

Lori turned to ask Ray, but he was still lost in the distance. He wouldn't know what she wanted. It would be only a guess. Hadn't he just lamented that he apparently didn't know his daughter at all?

"One conversation," Ray murmured. "What I wouldn't give for just one conversation. One question, even."

"There are always questions when someone dies."

Ray turned to her. "When your husband died?"

Lori had to admit that Glenn's death seventeen years ago didn't leave many unanswered questions. Although he hadn't been sick terribly long, she'd had a chance to settle things, say goodbye, get closure.

"For all we know, that was exactly why Debbie came back," Lori pointed out. "And she was killed before she got the chance."

Dimly, Lori remembered that yesterday, she'd wondered if Ray might have been capable of violence. Looking at this deflated, defeated dad, she knew he hadn't hurt his daughter. All he wanted from her was one answer, and surely if she'd come back here, she would have given him that.

"We'll never really know," he said darkly.

"No, we won't. Sometimes, we just have to choose the thing that gives us the most peace. The most hope."

He turned his faded blue eyes on her. "I've let hope fester for ten years, but now I see what a mistake it was. Hope is cruel."

Lori patted his wrist again and let the conversation lapse for a long time, sitting, suffering in silence until they heard stirrings from upstairs. Ray stood to go to his wife, and Lori stood to leave.

"Ray?" she said. He paused on the stairs. "We're going to find out who took her from you."

Ray simply nodded, numb again, and continued up the stairs.

She'd braced herself, Lori realized, for his argument—no one had taken Debbie. She'd left.

But she'd come back, and someone *had* taken her.

Lori locked the door behind her, vowing to herself: she would find out who had done this. Even if it meant Mitch or Chip went to jail for the rest of his life.

Chapter 10

Lori returned to the inn, determined to head straight to her office. She needed to make a list or something, try to organize and evaluate the evidence, figure out what she was overlooking. There had to be some clue or something she just hadn't noticed yet.

When she reached the kitchen, however, she remembered her other responsibilities. The joys of innkeeping. Her primary job, she reminded herself.

She stopped by the laundry room and gathered up the clean linens. With a quick folding session—a load of towels was only a couple minutes of work these days—she was ready to refresh her guests' rooms.

Lori changed out the towels downstairs first. The suite had been empty last night, but Adam would be arriving tonight. Normally, she was grateful for the help, even if her sons weren't working like hired housekeepers around the inn. But this weekend, she needed help of a different kind entirely, and she wasn't sure she wanted to involve her sons in that kind of work at all.

Lori carried the towels up past the main floor to the guest rooms upstairs. The Oak Island Room and Bald Head Island Suite didn't need new towels. Lori knocked at the door to the Carolina Beach Room. When there was no answer, she ducked in to change out the towels, make the bed and grab the trash bag, glad she'd filled the can with several liner bags so she didn't have to spend time changing that out. She deposited the trash—only brochures—in the trash bag in the linen closet, leaving the dirty towels on the cart for a moment while she visited the last two rooms.

Next, she knocked at the door to the Ocean Isle Beach Room. "Housekeeping."

"Just a minute," called a man from inside. Mr. Kirk, Lori reminded herself. Shawn, the one who was sad and had a tan line from his missing ring.

She'd hoped her chores would be quick, but this delay was already messing up her timeline. Lori tried to be patient as she waited for him, reminding herself that her grief—and Ray's and Katie's and Mitch's—wasn't the only one in the world. She wasn't sure she could really gain that much perspective, though, in the midst of a murder investigation and all the other emotional baggage that was coming with this one in particular.

When Shawn finally opened the door, she was hit with a strong smell of smoke. She tried to peer past him to find the source.

"Can I help you?"

Lori held up the towels. "Housekeeping."

"Right." He stepped back to let her in. Lori headed for the bathroom, still trying to surreptitiously check for something burning. There was a book on the table, not on fire, and the remnants of his dinner in the trash can, also not smoking. The microwave and minifridge seemed fine.

But the smoke wasn't a food smell or paper or wood or candle, Lori realized as she hung up the fresh towels. It was a harder, plastic smell. Had he tried reheating something in Styrofoam? She'd just added the small microwaves and fridges a month ago, and already they were causing problems.

Lori scooped up the dirty towels from the floor and hurried to toss them into the hall. As she turned back to the room, Shawn appeared behind her to close the door. Lori hopped back, startled. "Oh, I'm not quite finished."

Shawn's eyebrows lowered, but he stepped back again to let

her in. She quickly straightened the bed, which hardly looked slept in anyway, and grabbed the bag from the trash can.

"Uh—" Shawn started to reach for her, but Lori stepped back into the hall.

"Is there anything else I can do for you? Dinner arrangements?"

The look of discomfort on Shawn's face dissolved. "That would be great. Just something simple like a burger."

Lori smiled and retrieved the towels from the floor. "Cheese? Onions? Pickles?"

"All of the above. But no bun, obviously."

"I'll get right on that." Lori turned away but stopped short. "Oh, and just so you know, because of insurance, we can't have flames or fires of any kind in the guest rooms."

"Oh, yeah, sorry, I left lunch in the microwave a little too long." He gave a sheepish laugh.

"New microwaves." Lori gave him a what-can-you-do shrug and turned away. She'd have to write up instructions on using the microwaves when she got a spare minute. Could she stick them to the microwaves? The fridges? Should she laminate them?

Yep, just another joy of innkeeping.

Finally, she knocked at the Sunset Beach Room. "Housekeeping."

"Uh—come back later," called the guest. Jared Lehanneur, Lori reminded herself. Some relative of the former chief.

"Can I just give you some clean towels?" Lori offered.

The door flew open and Jared leaned out, far too close to Lori. She skittered back. Had she not been in close enough quarters with him before to notice his total lack of understanding of personal space and hospitality?

Lori chided herself. Few people lived in an inn full-time, and maybe Jared wasn't a big vacationer. She should work even harder to make sure he was comfortable. "Here you go," she said, offering the towels.

Jared snatched them. "Thanks. Do you have a do not disturb sign or something?"

She tried not to take offense. "It should be in the nightstand drawer. Can I take your dirty towels?"

He shut the door in her face. This time it was a little harder not to be offended, but the door swung open again and a towel flew out, hitting Lori in the face.

Jared didn't apologize and probably didn't notice, slamming the door shut again.

He was certainly in a hurry to get rid of her. Good thing she had lots of other things to be doing.

Lori pondered on the best way to put up instructions for the new appliances, grabbing the rest of the dirty towels and dropping them off in the washer. She wouldn't run it until the morning, just in case she ended up making any more laundry tonight. Seemed to be a bad habit—or an unlucky streak over the last year—whenever she started the washer, something else got dirty or stained immediately.

Once she was at her desk, she put in an order for a bun-free burger at Slush Puppy's and pulled out her trusty legal pad. At last.

What evidence did she have?

She'd seen the body. She couldn't tell what might or might not be evidence just by looking. Lori made a list of what she had noticed about Debbie's body. Black blouse with tiny blue flowers. Black pants. No shoes. Dark hair, possibly dyed, but it was hard to tell when it was wet. Ring on her left ring finger.

The doorbell rang in her office, and Lori sighed, setting aside the legal pad. Shawn's dinner was fast. Lori left her office and headed through the parlor to the front door, not bothering to check the peephole.

Chief Branson stood on her porch. When he saw her, he gathered up his weight and his breath and his belt, as if girding up his loins for hard work.

Or hard battle.

"Chip." Lori nodded to him, trying to keep her tone cordial while her mind raced back to yesterday at the police station. Where he'd intimidated her.

Was he here to do that again?

And hadn't Ray just told her he'd long believed Chip knew more about Debbie's disappearance than he was letting on?

"Can I come in?" he asked.

He actually asked. Lori couldn't remember perfectly right now, but it had seemed like most of the time, he'd pretty much demanded to come in, not waiting for an invitation.

Lori did the polite thing and moved out of the way. He stepped into the parlor and took the doorknob from her, pulling the door from her hands to shut it. "Are you busy?" he asked.

The legal pad flashed through her mind, and Lori measured Chip for a moment. He seemed calm, somber even. "No, not busy," she said.

"We need to talk."

Ice seemed to wash over Lori. Had something happened? One of her sons? Adam was on his way here right now.

Ray? Katie?

Mitch?

"What's the matter?" Lori asked, the fear bleeding into her voice.

"We need to talk about your . . . investigation," Chip said, as if choosing that last word with much care.

Oh. Lori pulled back before the relief even registered. "What about my investigation?"

"Lori." His voice held pity and empathy. "You've got to stop this."

"Stop what?"

"Stop pestering people about this. You're digging up old wounds."

Lori declined to point out the mixed metaphor. "It's not *my* fault things came to the surface again." She wasn't proud of her word choice, either.

"You're not helping," Chip said, his tone now gentle. "I know that's all you want to do, but you're just making it worse for us."

"'Us,' the police, or 'us,' you and somebody." She waved a hand to indicate that could mean anyone. Not Ray or Katie or

Kim specifically, even though they were the main ones she'd talked to.

"Both."

Lori looked away, trying to focus on her fireplace. She didn't particularly care if she was making it hard for the police, since she'd seen firsthand that they didn't particularly care about justice once they thought they had their man. But she wasn't trying to make life hard for Ray or Katie or Kim or Mitch or whoever.

When Lori's eyes settled on Chip again, she could tell she wasn't giving him the answers he wanted. The tight set of his jaw, his knuckles white as he gripped his belt below his belly. "Lori." Now her name sounded stern. "You've got to cut this out."

"I'm trying to help," she said again. "Ray and Katie deserve to know the truth."

"Yes, they do. Look, I've put up with you because you were helping, but this time you're just too biased to help with anything."

"Biased? Toward Ray and Katie?"

"Toward Mitch. Obviously."

Lori scoffed. "You're not biased this time?"

Chip's eyebrows crept higher. "Bias has nothing to do with it. Mitch did this."

"You can't prove that—again—and that isn't your job. That's for a court to decide." Some tiny corner of her brain sent up a prayer that when Mitch faced a court for the first time in the morning, the judge would throw out this ridiculous, nonexistent case. Or at least set bail.

"The court decides using the evidence we collect."

A chill ran through Lori again. That sounded almost like a threat. "What kind of evidence, then?" she demanded.

"I don't have to tell you that. I shouldn't."

Lori folded her arms and fixed him with a look of *you'd better tell me the truth, the whole truth, and nothing but the truth, young man.* "As far as I can see, there's as much reason to suspect you as there is Mitch."

His neck started turning pink above the collar again. Lori had never seen him lose his cool quite like this before this weekend, but she really didn't want a repeat of yesterday here, alone.

"You want evidence?" Chip released his belt and began to tick off items on his fingers. "One, how did you decide where to go crabbing?"

"I don't know. It was Mitch's choice."

"Wrong answer: it was Debbie's favorite spot."

Lori threw up her hands. "How on earth would I know that?"

"So Mitch picked the spot?"

She buttoned her lips. No more inadvertent evidence against him if she could help it. "How could you remember that, anyway?"

"Who do you think took her there first?"

Lori tried to picture the bridge fishing spot as somewhere for romance of any kind and failed utterly, miserably. Even her own proposal—if that was what it was at all—was only magical at the time because of the sunset and the company.

"We've searched his house." This time, his voice sounded like he was breaking bad news to her, as if she'd know exactly what that meant.

"And?"

Chip ticked off the next item on his fingers. "We found her diary from ten years ago. Paints Mitch in a pretty bad light."

"But he didn't kill her ten years ago. Obviously."

Chip ignored her, charging onward. "We also found her wedding ring in his nightstand."

"How do you know it was hers?" The question was out before she realized how ridiculous it sounded. But was the wedding ring Chip's rival gave his old flame really etched into the man's memory? Couldn't it have been the ring Mitch was about to give her?

If that was even the case.

"I know, Lori," Chip said in a low voice. She decided to concede that point and pretend her boyfriend wasn't keeping his not-really-late wife's ring as close as he could.

He shouldn't have been her boyfriend.

Chip wasn't finished. "His phone records showed that she called that morning."

"Did he answer?"

Chip, for one, didn't. "You think it's a coincidence he found her body?"

"Wouldn't it have been better to *not* find it? Or at least not with me?"

"You're the perfect alibi," Chip said. "If nothing else, you'd be the perfect witness because he knew you'd take it upon yourself to meddle in this and get him out of jail."

Lori fixed her eyes on his. "You didn't see him when he first saw her face. He didn't know she was in Dusky Cove."

Chip hung his head, but not in defeat. Like it pained him to tell her this. "Listen, Lori, I like you, despite everything. I think you're a good person. You don't deserve what he's putting you through at the very least."

She figured it was best not to thank him quite yet.

"You *do* deserve to know this. I'm telling you as someone who's worried about you: you've got to get out from under Mitch's spell as soon as you can."

Lori bit back a scoff, though some part of her certainly felt she'd been under Mitch's spell. She'd loved him, and he'd lied about—everything, about who he was.

"On his desk," Chip said slowly, carefully, "we found divorce papers."

The words plinked into her mind in silence at first, but within seconds, ten thousand questions thundered after them. Divorce papers. From Mitch? From Debbie? Dated when? Served? When? Signed? Finalized?

Her heart sent up a flare of hope, and Ray's words came echoing back to her.

It really was cruel.

Mitch couldn't be secretly divorced, Lori told herself. He'd told her he'd consulted a lawyer and hadn't mentioned that. Instead, she braced for the worst.

"What did the divorce papers tell you?" she asked, her tone flat, almost too detached.

Chip shifted, looking away form her. "We suspect that she'd tried to serve them to him. That was why she'd called, and why he hadn't answered."

"He didn't answer because he didn't know the number. Why would he think his dead wife wanted to get in touch?" Once the words were out, Lori realized her own mistake: Mitch knew she wasn't his *dead* wife.

"Obviously he knew she was in town," Chip said. "Or he figured it out pretty quick."

"Were the papers signed?" Lori asked.

Chip paused, thrown enough that he actually had to shift a step. "Were they signed?" he repeated.

Lori nodded. "If she served him with the papers, I'm assuming she'd already signed them?"

A flicker of concern—or maybe doubt—crossed Chip's face. "No. They weren't signed."

So much for that idea.

Chip reached out and patted her on the shoulder. As if this could be any more awkward, he let his hand rest there, uncomfortable for probably both of them. "I know this is hard. It's not what you want to believe about him."

Lori held up a hand, cutting him off and conveniently knocking his arm away from her shoulder. "I don't know what to believe about him anymore. Don't pretend like either of us do."

"Right." He fell back to a better distance, nodding. "I just . . . this isn't what I want, either."

"Oh no? You don't want to put Mitch away for Debbie's murder?"

"I want justice too." He shoved his hands in his pockets and cast his eyes toward the couch. Did he expect her to invite him in? Sit down and bond over their broken hearts? Lori was so caught up in preparing to shut down that idea that she almost missed what he said when he finally murmured, "But I'd rather have Debbie than justice."

Was that the way a man who'd murdered someone thought about his victim?

Maybe. Maybe if he'd killed her because she was rejecting him. But she'd known Chip for two years, and that didn't really seem like him, either.

A knock sounded at the door, and Lori stepped past Chip to check the peephole this time. A delivery man stood on the porch, holding a paper bag from Slush Puppy's.

Without a word, Lori opened the door. She accepted the delivery and paid with a tip—mentally noting the amount to charge to Shawn's room—and then opened the door wider.

Chip took the hint and walked out. She shut the door behind him and leaned against it for one minute.

Divorce papers. Had they come from Mitch? Or Debbie? She knew Mitch had consulted a lawyer, but he didn't say anything about actual papers. If Debbie had come to sign the papers, why would Mitch have been as surprised as he was when they found her? And why would he have killed her?

Or maybe she didn't want to sign.

Of course she did. She was wearing a wedding ring. She'd moved on, and so had Mitch.

But judging by the way he'd held her disappearance over Mitch for a decade, Chip had definitely *not* moved on.

Had Chip murdered Debbie? Somehow, it still felt like a stretch.

Then had Mitch killed her? Obviously he'd lied and covered up her death for eight years—and then dated Lori knowing Debbie was still alive. But was he really capable of murder?

Chapter 11

L ori delivered Shawn's dinner to his room and stopped by the office to make a note on his account.

She returned to the parlor, ready to sit down with her legal pad and walk through the evidence she'd collected and everything Chip had just told her, when footsteps sounded down the stairs. Lori turned to look: Jared had emerged from his room at last. She quickly flipped the legal pad facedown in her lap.

"Was that Chip Branson I just heard?"

He knew Chip? Oh, of course he did. "You're related to Chief Lehanneur, right?"

"So my mom tells me." He grinned, but when Lori didn't get the joke, he added, "He was my father."

She couldn't help an eyebrow jump. Here was someone else who might remember the first time Debbie went missing. "Do you remember when Debra Griffin went missing?"

"Debbie Watson?" Jared shook his head. "Sorry, I'd moved away by then. Sad, isn't it?"

Lori nodded slowly. Clearly he knew Debra, if he knew her nickname and maiden name. But apparently he wasn't going to be any help. "Are you headed out?" she asked. "Dinner?"

"Yes. Is anything still open in this town? Or have they already rolled up the sidewalks?"

She barely managed not to roll her eyes. "Try the Salty Dog or the Mimosa Café." Slush Puppy's was open, too, but she'd thrown enough business their way today.

Jared saluted and left. Lori turned back to her legal pad for less than a minute before yet another knock sounded at the door. With a sigh, Lori stuffed her legal pad in a drawer of the antique sideboard and answered the knock.

This time, the surprise on her front porch was a good one: her younger son, Adam, stood there, grinning broadly. "Hey, Mom! Younger and more beautiful than ever, I see."

She'd gotten so sidetracked with Chip and Mitch and investigating that she'd forgotten for a moment that he was coming tonight. She caught him up in a hug, then held him at arms' length. "You cut your hair!" she exclaimed.

Adam's grin turned sheepish, and he rubbed a hand over the buzzed cut, not much longer than the scruff on his face. Lori bit back her perennial question: why couldn't he shave properly?

That wasn't important right now. All that mattered was that he was here. "How was dinner at Sierra's house?"

"Her parents' house," he corrected. "It was good."

"And how's that big account coming?" Lori could never remember the potential client's name, but it was a subsidiary of 3M.

"The presentation for them is Tuesday." He held up crossed fingers.

"Are you ready?"

Adam grinned. "Of course. Enough about me. Ready to put me to work?"

Lori patted his shoulder, ready to dismiss his offer of help—dating the maintenance man meant that she was actually up-to-date on repairs now, at the start of the season. But that wouldn't be the case going forward.

Was it bad, though, that her most pressing concern wasn't the inn right now?

No, she was allowed to have a personal life, even if those could be very demanding sometimes. "I guess there is something you could help with," she told Adam at last.

He hefted his duffel bag and followed her in. "Name it."

"I'm investigating a murder."

Adam's brown eyebrows immediately knit together. "You're doing what?"

"I've told you about this before."

He shot her a look that was a perfect mix of concern and skepticism. "I thought you were giving that up."

"When did I say that?" But then Lori waved away her own question. She had to focus on what really mattered right now. "This time I don't have a choice."

"And you want my help?"

"I just need someone to talk through the case with. Bounce ideas off of."

Adam's shoulders dropped with his sigh. "Let me just set down my stuff. Downstairs again?"

"Yep."

Adam kissed her forehead and headed down the stairs. Lori retrieved her legal pad and a pen and settled on the couch.

But part of her knew that even talking this out with Adam wasn't going to help make anything right. That same part was pretty convinced that nothing would truly be right, not ever again.

Monday morning dawned bright and unsure for Lori. Mitch should have his bail set today, but she now wasn't sure that was a good thing.

She needed to ask him about the divorce papers, find out what he knew. But after their last conversation, she still wasn't sure she wanted to speak to him. Ever.

Lori put on the most business-y thing she had, a drape-front cardigan in a bright yellow that still managed to make her look professional and put-together. For a split second, she remembered how paranoid she'd been about her appearance for so long, certain she could never pull off something like this. What a difference a year could make.

Adam had gotten up early—he had always been an early riser—and made his famous Liège-style waffles with the chunks of pearl sugar in them. Her guests would think she'd been holding out on them if she served the best breakfast on their last morning. She joined him in the kitchen to cut up fruit and whip up cream—and find a gluten-free option for Shawn. Their small talk neatly avoided the case, which felt just as impenetrable as it had last night.

"What are you going to do today?" Adam's words seemed to echo in the kitchen. His tone made it clear that he wasn't casually asking about her plans—he wanted to know what decision she'd make about the question hanging over her.

Would she go to watch Mitch's arraignment?

"I don't know," she murmured. Did she want to know what plea he would enter?

Did she still think he might have done this?

Lori frowned, scooping the whipped cream into a serving bowl. She didn't think he'd done it, but she still wasn't sure whether that was because of her investigation sense or because she really didn't want him to be a murderer.

Even if she did go and listen to Mitch plead not guilty—obviously—there was no guarantee the judge would let him out on bail. He could just as easily end up right back in the cell where he sat now.

"What do you think I should do?" Lori asked.

Adam cast a quick glance at her, his eyebrows quirked. Point taken: when was the last time she'd asked her youngest for advice?

"I don't know, Mom. If everything goes as good as it possibly could, would you regret going or not going?"

Things going as good as possible would require time travel at this point, to make it so she wasn't dating a married man. And in that alternate reality, yes, she'd regret not being at the arraignment.

After a pause, Adam continued: "If everything goes as bad as it possibly could, which would you regret?"

The worst-case scenario would be Mitch pleading guilty. And honestly, she'd want to be there to see that, too, to know for herself, to watch his body language, to be sure he was telling the truth.

Then it seemed settled. "Good questions, Adam."

"Thanks. I learned from the best."

Lori laughed. Surely he didn't mean her? If that were true, she would have had this whole case tied up by now.

Adam helped her prep a few more quick items: hard-boiled eggs and yogurt parfaits again for Shawn, and another fruit salad, and they made sure the dining room was guest-ready.

"When are you leaving?" Adam asked after he finished counting the forks.

"Who said I'm going anywhere?" Lori asked, half-teasing.

"Mom." He set down the handful of spoons. "I've seen you two together. You love him. He loves you. I know he screwed up, but if he didn't do this and you believe that, then maybe he deserves a second chance."

Lori pondered his words a moment, creasing and recreasing the napkin in her hands. "Maybe" was the best she could give him.

It was the best she could give Mitch right now, too. She was pretty sure she hadn't even hit rock bottom in the process of grieving for their relationship, her image of Mitch, and his integrity. She still didn't know what the future would hold for either of them.

"You're going, right?" Adam asked at last.

"Yes," Lori said with more conviction than she felt.

Going to the arraignment didn't mean she was going to give Mitch a ride home and a key to the inn, although he had kept one for her from time to time. She didn't have to see or talk to him. She'd just sit in the back of the gallery and wait to see the results.

Lori repeated that mantra to herself throughout breakfast. Shawn was as melancholy as ever, enough that Lori almost felt guilty for insisting on charging him and making him stay. Jared didn't warm up until he'd had three cups of coffee, and then he chattered nonstop with the Besases, who were their usual selves, happy and enthusiastic and bright. Even Shawn seemed to perk up while they were in the room.

Lori and the Besases convinced Jared to get out and head to the beach. The Besases were going to check out the museum and the colonial fort. Lori volunteered to hold onto their bags for them, since they had to check out now. Adam patted her shoulder, as if silently assuring her he could handle checkout.

Once breakfast was over and the dishes assembled in the kitchen, Adam practically shooed her out the door. "I've got this, Mom."

She smiled back at her son. He'd always been her baby, and sometimes she forgot how grown-up he was now. For a moment, she just took him in, this adult stranger that somehow she'd brought into the world, now here to help her out in a way that no one else could.

"Thank you," she said at last.

"Of course, Mom. Now go!"

Lori reminded herself over and over again that she didn't have to talk to Mitch or even make eye contact. He didn't even need to know she was there, depending on how big the courtroom was. With a little help from guards in the courthouse, she found the right spot—there weren't that many courtrooms to choose from. It was already nearly eleven o'clock. Had they already arraigned Mitch? Lori scanned the courtroom. He was nowhere in sight.

She glanced around the gallery, in case anyone else from Dusky Cove might have come out for this. Mitch wasn't without friends, although given the circumstances, who knew what they might think of him now?

Of course, if his case had already been heard, any friends probably wouldn't stick around afterwards.

The first person she recognized in the gallery was Curtis Hopkins, Andrea's husband and the editor of the *Dusky Chronicle*. The overhead lights shone off his bald head, the glare a sharp contrast from his deep brown skin. He'd definitely know if Mitch had been through yet. Lori moved to a seat next to him.

"Hey, Lori," he greeted her. "Do I even need to ask why you're here?"

"I'm sure you've already guessed the reason. Have they arraigned him yet?"

Curtis shook his head. "Rumor has it the judge will deny bail."

Lori twisted her lips together. Angry as she was with him, she really didn't think Mitch deserved to stay in jail for a crime he didn't commit.

Curtis pointed across the courtroom with his pen. Lori followed the direction. A door to the side of the courtroom had opened, and in marched Mitch in handcuffs.

Everything about this felt wrong, more twisted and tortured than living in a fun house mirror. Lori wasn't sure the feeling came from seeing someone that she hadn't stopped loving—yet?— who'd done something wrong by dating her when he was married, or from seeing someone who she knew was a good and most likely innocent person in shackles.

Mitch took a seat in the waiting area at the side of the courtroom, his eyes down. Slowly, they called up each of the other prisoners assembled there, read off their crimes, let the judge set their bail. One person pled guilty and got off with a fine.

Didn't seem likely for Mitch.

Finally, it was Mitch's turn. He was marched to the front of the courtroom, his lawyer standing by him.

Lori could only manage shallow breaths as they read off the charges.

Mitch—really, his lawyer—pled not guilty.

Lori gripped the bench on either side of her, almost as tight as she had that night when they were in the boat.

Right before they found Debbie's body.

"Bail is set at one million dollars," the judge proclaimed. Lori forgot how to breathe for a few seconds.

A million dollars? Her own bail—also for murder—had been less than a quarter of that, and she was pretty sure inflation hadn't been quite that bad in the last two years.

How would they—er, just Mitch—afford even the partial deposit required?

Curtis gave a low whistle barely loud enough for Lori to hear. "Still got off lucky, though. I'd hate to be in his shoes."

Lori huffed out a bitter laugh. She'd been there, and she never wanted it to happen to her or anyone she cared about again.

Mitch was ushered out of the courtroom.

"Wait," Lori said. "Did he say he was going to post bail?"

"Yes."

She relaxed for a moment. She didn't know how he was going to come up with that, but at least she knew the outcome.

He'd pled not guilty.

He was coming home.

Lori thanked Curtis and left the courtroom. The whole drive back to the inn, she debated. Mitch would be home in a couple hours. Should she go see him? Was she ready for that? He hadn't seen her in the courtroom, right?

No, she decided, to all three questions. She wasn't ready to see him, so she wouldn't. And she was pretty sure he hadn't seen her.

That meant he wouldn't know that she'd gone to support him.

Did he need to know? Did she want him to?

Lori reviewed the people she'd seen in the courtroom. As she'd waited for Mitch's turn, she couldn't help but notice Curtis was the only other one there from Dusky Cove.

Mitch needed to know someone believed him. Even if she wasn't totally sure about that sometimes.

By the time Lori reached the inn, she knew what she needed to do: express her love language—food. She had this one recipe that Mitch really loved, bless his heart for loving sweet corn anything.

Lori had always preferred her cornbread the classic Southern corn pone way her grandmother had made it: cornmeal with buttermilk until it looked right, salt until it tasted right and baked in a cast iron skillet until it looked done. The bottom was usually burnt, and the texture was strange to someone who hadn't grown up with it, but it was Lori's acquired taste. Any amount of sugar in her cornbread was anathema.

But she'd tried a honey cornmeal cake to see if her guests would prefer that to her grandmother's recipe—yes—and Mitch had fallen in love with it.

She arrived back at the inn to find the Besases' checkout managed perfectly, their bags waiting in her office, and the kitchen sparkling. Adam was hard at work updating a marketing campaign on Facebook—something Lori would never understand but was more than grateful for his help with.

"How'd it go?" Adam asked, his voice a little tight with nerves.

"High bail," Lori said, "but he got bail."

"Good. Right?"

Lori nodded slowly, almost absently. She really didn't like not knowing the answer to that question.

"What should we do for lunch?" Adam asked, but his grin said he already knew the answer: Brunswick stew and hush puppies from the Salty Dog.

Of course. Food was always the answer. That was exactly what she should do. "I'm going to make him a welcome home treat first," Lori decided.

Adam quirked an eyebrow but didn't question her choice out loud.

Lori headed for her comfort zone, her kitchen, and dug the recipe out of the rack of cookbooks. She assembled the ingredients. For some strange reason, the recipe had her flour the pan with cornmeal. Effective for pizzas, perhaps, but it had worked the last time she'd made this, so she went with it. The batter was equal parts cornmeal, butter, sugar and eggs, with a little sour cream, vanilla and flour to round it out.

Baking wasn't really the distraction she'd hoped for, but Lori forced herself to focus only on how the butter and sugar creamed together, how the texture changed with the eggs and dry ingredients, making sure each step was perfect.

Unlike each step of her investigation. Every time she'd found a suspect, she'd found four reasons to believe their innocence.

And then there was the evidence against Mitch that Chip had listed off last night. The journal she already felt she understood, but the divorce papers, the ring . . .

Wait. The ring? Lori poured the batter into the prepared pan, but her mind was fixed on the ring.

She'd seen a ring on Debbie's left ring finger. It was one of the first things she noticed.

And one of Mitch's reasons that he knew she wasn't dead, that she'd left of her own volition: she'd left her ring.

Of course Mitch had it. He'd had it for ten years.

He'd told her he'd been seeing a lawyer. The papers had to be ones he'd prepared, even if he had no idea how to get them served.

All of Chip's "hard evidence" evaporated like steam. Lori slid the cake pan into the hot oven. With a burst of energy she whipped up—literally, by hand—the honey glaze for the top of the cake.

Mitch hadn't done this. Mitch was innocent.

Lori finished the glaze in two minutes flat, and her enthusiasm instantly waned. None of that changed what Mitch had done to her, of course.

"Hey, Mom?" Adam called, heading into the kitchen.

"Yes?"

"Your guest for tonight had their flight delayed. They probably won't get to Wilmington before ten thirty." It was another forty-five minutes to the inn from there, plus time to get baggage and a rental car. They could be arriving after midnight.

"Do you want me to stay to greet them?" Adam offered.

To think she'd ever believed, even for a minute, that he would have resented helping with the inn. "No, sweetie. We use a lockbox for after-hours check-ins."

"I don't mind. I'd already be up."

He was supposed to head home tonight. "Don't you have work tomorrow?"

Adam shrugged. "I can take it off."

"And miss your big presentation? No." She patted his shoulders. "I appreciate it, but I've got systems to handle this already. You're heading back home tonight."

"All right. Show me how this lockbox works?"

Lori squeezed his shoulder. They'd get the keys set up for the guest, get the cake over to Mitch, and get the housekeeping done in record time.

Chapter 12

No one was home when Lori stopped by Mitch's house. Not that she knocked, but the house seemed quiet. His SUV was out front where it had been all weekend. Lori left the cake on a chair on his porch and hurried back to the inn with Brunswick stew and hush puppies from the Salty Dog for her and Adam to share.

Adam spent most of lunch talking about marketing efforts for the inn. Half the time it almost seemed like this was a job interview. As if she could afford to hire a full-time marketer.

Perhaps he was merely nervous about his presentation tomorrow.

Finally, as he sopped up the last of his tomato-based stew with half a hush puppy, Adam asked a question that had clearly been on his mind the whole meal. "Did you see him?"

Lori just shook her head.

"And how do you feel about that?"

She pondered the question for a moment. "Fine, I guess. It was hard to see him this morning at the courthouse, even if I didn't have to talk to him."

"Because you still love him."

Lori turned to look out the windows. All she could see from here were the dark windows of Dusky Card and Gift.

She wasn't doing enough to help Ray and Katie, and she'd run out of leads. Even going over everything with Adam, who was hopefully more impartial than she was, they'd cast legitimate doubts on Ray, Chip and Mitch as the murderer.

"The investigation isn't about me," she finally murmured.

"But bringing him a welcome-home treat certainly was."

Lori had to acknowledge her son's point. Leaving a treat was an easy way to say, *Hey, I'm still thinking about you, even if I'm not sure that will ever be in a romantic way again, you big fat liar.*

On second thought, maybe a cake didn't say "you big fat liar."

"Mom," Adam said, drawing her attention back to him. "You're hurting right now, but I think your heart is already trying to tell you what you should do long-term. It might take a while to rebuild trust, but you know what you want."

"What I want is for none of this to have ever happened." Her laugh sounded cold and bitter to her own ears. "But I'm obviously not getting what I want. Until we figure out who did kill Debbie, everyone is going to think Mitch did it." And honestly, until he could be ruled out definitively, she'd have her doubts, too.

Or was that just because she was angry that he'd dated her while he'd known Debbie was alive?

Adam offered a half-frown. "I'm sorry, Mom. I know it hurts now."

She patted his hand, then stood to clear his place, but Adam hopped to his feet and grabbed both of their bowls before she could.

"I see someone taught you well."

"She sure did," Adam called over his shoulder on his way to the kitchen. "Housekeeping now?"

Lori nodded. Together, they retrieved clean sheets and towels from the dryer. Adam headed downstairs to change his own room over for her, while Lori started with the towels.

Her sweeps of the rooms yesterday had been so fast they almost hadn't counted, although she wouldn't have been changing sheets or deep cleaning in a guest's room during the middle of a weekend stay. Today, they'd have to change bedding in the Besases' room as well as do another quick refresh of Shawn's and Jared's rooms.

She changed out the towels and collected the trash from the

empty guest rooms first. Leaving the bedding and cleaning for Adam to start. Jared's room went quickly—nothing seemed unusual, so she wasn't sure why he'd been so cagey yesterday.

When she stopped to get the trash bag, however, she noticed the book on the table—a high school yearbook. It was open to a two-page spread of students wearing tuxes and black evening dresses. Seniors, in the second half of the alphabet. A few faces looked vaguely familiar, and then Lori saw the most familiar of all: Debra Watson. Her quote was simply "Carpe diem." Next to it was a handwritten note: *Jared, You're a great friend! Whoever gets you is a lucky girl. Have fun in college! Your friend, Deb.*

Calling him a friend twice in a short message was interesting. It almost sounded like she was trying to send him a subtle message.

Debbie must have been the most popular girl in school if she had three friends competing for her attention. Lori looked at her photo again, trying to ignore a twinge of jealousy.

"Mom?" Adam called. "What are you doing?"

She glanced at the yearbook once more. "Nothing." She held up the trash bag and headed out.

Adam carried the linens downstairs, and Lori found herself facing Shawn's door.

Every time she spoke to the poor boy, it seemed, he got sadder. She hoped he was still out now. Who went on a vacation to just sit around a stuffy historic home the whole time?

Lori knocked and waited, counting the seconds. After fifteen, there was no answer. Lori tried again. "Housekeeping?" she called through the door.

Again, no answer. Lori unlocked the room door and let herself in. A hint of the acrid smell of smoke still lingered from yesterday. Lori hurried to change the towels, then she checked the trash can quickly. Underneath the take out container from last night's dinner and a few used tissues, she found flaky ashes.

He'd burned something after she told him not to? Lori's brow furrowed in consternation as if her own son had disobeyed her direct order. She tried to be as accommodating as possible, but this was no way for a guest to behave. He easily could have started a fire, burning something in the trash.

Lori snatched out the bag and took it to the cart. Shawn's trash can was now out of bags, so she grabbed a roll of garbage liners from the linen closet. When she reached the room again, she took a deep breath.

Something about this smoke seemed a little different than yesterday, though. It wasn't quite the burning plastic smell that had assaulted her. This could be the smell from burning these papers today.

Lori refilled the trash can with empty bags. As she straightened, her eye caught the small microwave. She crossed the room to the appliance and pushed the button. The door sprang open, revealing the interior of the microwave before she even had a chance to brace herself.

The off-white enamel was as clean as the day she'd bought it.

She slammed the microwave closed and hurried out of the room without even turning the bed down.

It didn't look as though anything had melted in there. She'd specifically told him not to burn things in his room—which he'd obviously ignored. Why lie to her? It wasn't like he'd get in trouble.

Depending on what he was burning.

It didn't smell like drugs, from what Lori remembered of high school. She'd found ashes that looked like paper in the trash, but it didn't smell like that either. And that was from today's trash, but the smell had been there yesterday.

What about yesterday's garbage?

Lori headed back to the linen closet and pulled out the top trash bag. She hurried to untie the knot in the top and sifted through the trash to find the ashes again. The flakes were large and blackened and heavier than a regular sheet of paper. She pulled out the biggest one and held it at all angles, twisting it in the light and even holding it up. No text seemed to show up.

Of course not. This was silly.

The case was clearly getting to her. She was reading too

much into everything now, desperate for someone else to blame for Debbie's death.

The answer shouldn't be this complex. It should be simpler. Someone who'd known Debbie ten, twenty, thirty years ago. Not this random stranger staying in her inn.

Despite her mental protests, Lori found herself pulling the smaller, full trash bags out of the bigger bin, digging for the bag she'd removed from Shawn's room yesterday. Finally, she found it, with the Styrofoam takeout container stuffed inside—and something else.

She pulled out the knot pinning the Styrofoam inside and dumped that into the larger trash bin. Underneath were another few tissues, napkins, a wet wipe and a waterlogged book.

That was it? What had he burned yesterday, then? Lori turned back to the trash bin.

The Styrofoam container. He'd claimed he'd scorched it in the microwave. Maybe that wouldn't have left a mark or any melted remains. She picked up the takeout container and turned it over. Both the top and the bottom looked just fine.

She turned it back to toss it in the trash, but something shifted inside the box, hitting the side. Lori flipped open the lid.

Inside the box, amid the leftover rice and red sweet and sour sauce, lay a blackened and partially melted photograph. Lori turned it over to see the front.

It was a photograph of a dark-haired woman wearing sunglasses. Lori couldn't see quite enough of her face to recognize her, but she seemed familiar . . .

That couldn't be Debbie, could it? If it was, she looked more like the yearbook photo than the flyer Chip had given her. And the background certainly looked like Dusky Cove's beach.

"Hey!" came a man's voice. Lori startled, dropping the photo back in the sauce and tossing it into the trash. Had Shawn seen?

Lori whirled around toward the voice.

"Find something good, Mom?" Adam asked, walking up behind her. "Or . . . TMI?"

Her mind took a moment to latch onto Adam there, what he

was asking. "Oh, no. It was just . . . trash." She thought.

He lifted an eyebrow but accepted her answer. "Are these the right ones?" He held up the clean sheets in his arms.

"Yes." Lori pointed at the empty guest room they needed to turn over, and Adam headed away to take care of it.

She turned back to the trash bin. What did the photograph mean? Could it really be Debbie?

There wasn't enough of her face showing to really be sure, even if she showed the photo to Mitch. They certainly hadn't found her in sunglasses, but that would be pretty strange if they had.

On autopilot, Lori reloaded the trash bags into the bin. She grabbed her pile of dirty towels and carried them down to the laundry room, tossing them in the washer with the ones Adam had collected. The sheets would take a full load by themselves.

This wasn't making sense. How could Shawn have known Debbie? Why would he have a photograph of her? What did that mean for her investigation?

Lori paced the little laundry room for a minute. If only there were some way she could find out more about Shawn without him knowing she was prying. More photos, that was all she needed. Could she take his phone and see if he had any on there?

Unlikely. Where else might she find pictures of him and his friends?

Of course: the answer was right under her nose. Adam had coaxed her to set up a profile on Facebook largely so she could see pictures of what he and Doug were up to. If Shawn was on the social network, she could see his pictures, too, right?

She hurried to her office and her computer. Facebook pulled up quickly and Lori searched for Shawn Kirk. Three profiles popped up right away. Lori pulled up Shawn's check-in records to find his hometown. Atlanta.

Where Debbie had run away to. Coincidence?

Too soon to say. Atlanta was a huge city. They could live their all their lives and never meet.

Still, it wasn't exactly clearing her suspicions.

Lori switched back to the browser window with Facebook. One Shawn Kirk was from "Hotlanta." The picture was too small to make out.

She clicked on the profile, and it opened up. The main picture was of a silhouetted couple in a sunset. Could have been him and his ex-wife, or a stock photo.

Lori puffed out a breath. This wasn't helping. She found the Photos section on the page, but when they opened, nothing displayed. He had no photos? At all?

Adam breezed into the office, scaring her just a little bit less this time than he had upstairs. "Need anything else?"

Lori glanced at him—her personal Internet marketing guru. "What does it mean if somebody doesn't have any pictures on Facebook?"

"That they don't like pictures?" Adam guessed, like he was trying to solve an obscure riddle. He crossed the room and leaned over her. "Isn't this one of your guests?"

"I think so, but I'm not sure. That's why I wanted to see his photos."

Why couldn't she tell Adam the truth?

Because the truth was silly and hard to believe. She'd snooped in the trash and found a mostly-burned photo that bore a tiny resemblance to a dead woman she'd seen for only a few minutes. The last time she'd stretched logic this far, it had come back to bite her. Almost literally, with a gigantic dog attached. She'd been lucky to come out of it with only a broken foot.

"Are you friends with him yet?" Adam asked.

"No."

"You should add him as a friend and invite him to like the inn's page."

Lori nodded, as if she had any idea how to do that.

When she hesitated, Adam leaned in to take over. He tugged the mouse from her fingers and navigated back to Shawn's profile page. He clicked the button to Add Friend. "There. Now he just has to accept your request."

"How long will that take?"

"Depends." Adam shrugged. "Does he have a smartphone?"

Lori couldn't recall seeing Shawn's phone. "I'm not sure."

"Did he bring his laptop?"

She hadn't searched his room or anything—should she try that now? She hadn't seen a laptop sitting out. Really, she couldn't be sure whether he owned one. "I don't think so."

"Then it might not happen until he gets home. But he'll get an email telling him you requested him, and he'll accept it. I hope." Adam held up crossed fingers, and Lori mimicked the gesture. "I really want to get our Likes up."

Again, Lori pretended she had some clue what this meant. If circumstances were different, she might ask him to explain, but right now she was a little preoccupied.

"I'm going to go pack up," Adam said, dropping a quick kiss on the top of Lori's head. "You're sure you don't need me to stay?"

"No," Lori said, though she really couldn't be sure of anything at this rate. "You're good to go. Important client tomorrow," she reminded him.

Adam smiled, clearly touched that she'd remembered his schedule. That was all anyone really wanted, wasn't it? To be remembered?

Wouldn't Debbie want to be remembered?

Adam jogged from the office, leaving Lori to ponder the computer monitor. How long until Shawn accepted? What would she do if she found pictures of Debbie on his profile? Go to the police?

Nothing seemed to feel right. Even cooking didn't sound like it would help.

Lori knew she was just grasping at straws, anything to avoid the obvious-yet-impossible conclusion that Mitch, or maybe Chip, had killed Debbie. And still, she couldn't get her mind off this possibility.

She checked her Facebook every three minutes, as if Shawn would add her while he was finally out and about and enjoying his vacation for the first time.

Because he'd spent the rest of the time moping in his room.

Could his melancholy have to do with Debbie's death?

Lori looked at his photos again, his ex-wife still smiling out at her. Of course he was sad after his divorce. Besides, if being sad made you a murder suspect, then Mitch and Chip and Ray and half the town belonged on the suspect list.

Still. She needed hard evidence. And even the photograph wasn't enough—the photo.

Lori hopped up from her chair, but before she made it to the stairs, the front door opened. She froze. Was this Shawn returning? Was she too late to grab the photo from the trash bin upstairs without being discovered?

"Okay, Mom," Adam said, closing the door behind him. Goodness gracious, how many times was he going to accidentally scare her out of her skin before he left? He crossed the room to her. "Everything all right?"

Did she not look all right? She forced herself to nod. "Mm hm."

She should tell Adam about her suspicions.

But then he'd stay, probably for nothing, because this really was far-fetched. And he'd miss his big presentation tomorrow.

"Well, I'd better hit the road. Sierra made dinner plans for us."

Lori smiled. "Okay, sweetie. Drive safe."

"Always." He kissed the top of her head again.

"No speeding, no drowsy driving, and no texting and driving." Her usual admonishments had only required a little updating for this century.

Adam chuckled. "I'm a grown man, Ma."

"And I'm still your mother."

He gave her a quick squeeze. "I'll be back in a couple weeks, okay?"

"Thank you. I really appreciate your help."

"Well, I'll get on Doug's case to see if we can get him out here, too." Now that he finally lived within a reasonable driving distance, that actually looked like a possibility.

One last time, Lori considered telling Adam to stay, just in case that one blackened photograph of a dark-haired woman happened to be the same dark-haired woman at the center of the town's biggest controversies for the last ten years.

And one last time, she reminded herself that Adam had important reasons to leave that were far more concrete than her hunches.

She bid Adam goodbye, wishing that she believed herself half as much as she insisted she did.

Chapter 13

Lori returned to her office, pacing a small circle around the room. What was she supposed to do? Wait for Shawn to accept her request before she could snoop through his photos?

She didn't have time to wait around. Maybe there was a more direct way to find out about a relationship. Lori pulled out her cell phone and called Chip's number.

"Lori?" he answered, his voice weary already.

What was she supposed to say to him? *I found a photo that looks vaguely like Debbie in the trash of a man who as far as I know has no more connection to her than a few million other people?*

She opted for vagueness as the best policy. "Chip, hi. We have a bit of a situation down here. Can you come?"

"I'll send Eddie—"

"This is bigger than that. You need to come."

There was a half-second of pause. "Lights and sirens?" He sounded like he was already moving.

That would surely spook Shawn. "No, better not."

"On my way."

If he was coming here directly, it should only take about six minutes. But with the nervous energy caroming off the walls of her mind, Lori couldn't just sit in the parlor and wait. Besides, she had cleaning to do. The Vecchios were checking in tonight.

Lori headed back up the stairs and grabbed the cleaning supplies from the linen closet. She dragged the cart and vacuum down the hall. She wouldn't have time to vacuum before Chip got there, but she'd have to do it soon anyway.

Lori started with a quick wipe down of the nightstands, dressers and table with a disinfecting cloth. Definitely didn't want anyone getting sick from her inn. By the time she finished that, a knock sounded at the door.

Lori hurried back down the stairs to answer the door. Chip hurried past her, one hand on his hip—no, on his gun. He craned his neck around the room. "Where is he?"

He was ready to take Shawn down already? She hadn't even conclusively proved it was him yet—or even that he knew Debbie. "He's not here."

Chip's shoulders fell. "You said I needed to come down personally. Did you let him leave?"

"He's free to go," Lori said slowly. "And I didn't know what he'd done this morning."

"Everyone knew this morning—wait, Mitch?"

Lori shook her head vehemently. "No, my guest, of course."

Chip pressed his lips into a frustrated frown. "What's this about your guest?"

"Wait—maybe we should talk about Mitch first."

The police chief folded his arms, waiting for her to go on, if not entirely receptively.

"You came by and laid out the evidence against him the other day, right?"

He gave a single curt nod, then relaxed his arms to tick the items off on his fingers again: "Wedding ring, divorce papers, journal, phone call."

"Right. Would it surprise you that Mitch told me over the weekend that Debbie left the wedding ring behind when she left him? Before you mentioned the ring to me?"

Chip blinked, just shy of rolling his eyes. "Nothing would surprise me about this case anymore. I'm sure he realized we'd found the ring."

"And did you find the ring that was on her hand when we pulled her from the water? Her *left* hand?"

That one gave Chip a moment's pause. "He probably put it on her after he killed her."

She pursed her lips as if to ask *seriously?* "Seems like a stretch. Why wouldn't he use the first ring if he still had it?"

"I'm saying *she* had it, and he must have felt she didn't deserve it." At Lori's mystified look, Chip added, "He took it off her."

And hid it in his house? Once again, the chief was sounding just a little too much like someone who might have had a reason to hurt Debbie. Enough of a reason to actually do it.

And plenty of access to the evidence to make it look like Mitch was guilty.

"I'm guessing you've got rationale for dismissing the rest of the evidence, too," Chip said.

Although he obviously didn't want to hear about it, Lori nodded. "The journal was already a known quantity. Kim Yates read it years ago. She thought it meant Debbie had committed suicide."

He cocked an eyebrow. "You expect me to believe Kim Yates sat on the juiciest gossip of her life?"

"For her best friend? Stranger things have happened."

Chip drew a heavy sigh. "And the divorce papers?"

"He told me yesterday he was working with a lawyer."

The chief pinched the bridge of his nose, slowly shaking his head. "Look, Lori, you're a very nice person, and I know you mean well—"

"But I definitely don't know what I'm talking about when it comes to murders, so I should button my trap and butt out?" She let her sarcasm show how seriously she'd take that advice.

"Okay, yes, you've had a good streak. But that's not a replacement for serious investigation."

"Let me know when you start doing that, and I'll step out of the way." As soon as the words passed her lips, Lori clapped a hand over her mouth. "I'm sorry, I didn't—"

Chip just leveled her with a glower. "I was trying to give you a compliment. When it comes down to it, you're too biased to see

Mitch for who he is."

"And you aren't, with your high school grudge? When it comes to Debbie?"

Once again, pink began to creep up Chip's neck.

Lori held up a hand, cutting off their argument. "This isn't why I called you down here."

"Oh?"

"I found something today that I think you should see." She beckoned for him to follow her upstairs, and he did, no less grumpily than he'd listened to her rebuttal of the evidence.

Lori showed him upstairs to the linen closet. When she opened the door, Chip snorted behind her. "You wanted to show me cleaning supplies?"

She shot him a quick glare, then turned back to the closet, pulling trash bags out of the larger bin. After two or three, she spotted the Styrofoam container and pulled it out.

"Please don't tell me you're going to complain about something your guest ate."

She turned up the strength on her glare, then flipped open the box. She lifted the blackened photo from the sweet and sour sauce, its edges warped from the moisture.

Chip fell silent, leaning in and squinting at the photo. "You're telling me you think . . . you think that's Debbie?"

"Don't you?" Lori glanced down at the photo and remembered her own doubts.

"You can't see most of her face. Her hair's the right color, but it could be anybody with dark brown hair." Chip sighed like he was really, really sad for her. "Lori, you're grasping at straws. You know this isn't evidence."

Right, and that was why she'd tried to get a peek at Shawn's Facebook photos, but that hadn't panned out.

"I've known Deb our whole lives," he said, obviously using his practiced, patient police tone. "Even I couldn't tell if that's her. Can you?"

Her eyes flitted back to the photo again, but her hesitation was answer enough.

"Well?" Chip pressed.

"No," she admitted. "But it was enough to investigate."

"Uh huh. All those investigation skills we obviously don't have."

She needed to learn not to tick Chip off. It always came back to bite her.

"All right. If you find some actual evidence, call me, okay?"

"Yeah." Lori closed the Styrofoam container and dumped it back in the trash, piling the bags on top of it again. Maybe she was just lucky Shawn hadn't caught her looking at a photo that could be his mom or grandma. She didn't make eye contact with Chip as she led him back down the stairs.

Normally, her pride wasn't too wounded by the police—easy to let everything slide off your back when your first run-in was your own arrest for a murder you didn't commit—but today was different. So as Lori and Chip reached the ground floor of the inn, she stumbled upon a perfect, terrible, very wrong thing to say. She showed him to the door and opened it, standing there a moment.

"You knew Debbie your whole life?" she asked once he'd passed the threshold.

Chip turned back on the porch. "Better than anyone."

Lori paused and turned to him. "Then you know where she's been for the last ten years?"

This time, the pink didn't creep up from his collar: it flooded his face. Flustered, he floundered for words.

And Lori calmly closed the door in his face, not even giving him the satisfaction of answering the question for him.

As soon as the door shut, Lori kicked herself again. She really didn't mean to make a habit of investigating murders, but if this kept happening to her, she also really didn't want the chief of police to hate her.

Maybe a little too late for that.

Lori checked her watch. Surely her guests would be home soon. She took the photo to her office and wiped off the sweet and sour sauce before she hurried back upstairs and threw herself into cleaning.

She dust mopped the floor and wiped down the bathroom surfaces, telling herself that Chip had to be right. If not about Mitch, then definitely about the picture of Debbie. It could be anyone. Apparently anyone *but* her.

But if Chip could dismiss her concerns because of how she'd felt about Mitch, surely she could dismiss Chip's concerns because of how he'd felt about Debbie, right?

Of course right.

Although she had to admit she didn't have much evidence of anything concrete. Shaky at best. At worst, Chip was right.

But he was wrong about Mitch. He had to be.

Lori scrubbed out the toilet and swept the floor, taking the fluffy bathmat out to the hall for its turn in the laundry when she was done. She glanced down the hall to where Shawn's door still stood closed.

What *did* she know about the man? He lived in Atlanta. He was sad. He was probably divorced. He was on vacation alone.

Lori returned to the Carolina Beach Room and double-checked the closet and drawers, as well as the lamps and clocks, then ran the vacuum. Shawn had checked in Thursday. He hadn't seemed unhappy then. In fact, he was . . . jittery. She'd figured it was a long drive that had required caffeine, or had just made him a little stir-crazy.

Friday morning at breakfast, however, he was jittery even before his coffee, his hands shaking as he served himself breakfast and filled his mug. But he hadn't looked particularly sad at that point.

In fact, she couldn't remember the mournful look to his eyes before Friday evening.

Lori realized she'd stopped cleaning long ago and forced herself to put away the cart. Dusting wasn't quite distraction enough to keep her from recounting every conversation with Shawn.

At check-in, he was asking about good places to fish—no, originally he'd asked about places to sit and talk. He was excited;

his eyes didn't carry some hidden light, but something about him seemed . . . hopeful.

Friday at breakfast, he'd mentioned going fishing and looking for good spots. Lori told him he'd probably need a boat to access some of them—and he'd asked about renting one.

And then she'd told him about Miller's Point, where she and Mitch were going crabbing that night.

The spot that was Debbie's favorite as a teenager.

The place her body was found that night.

Goose bumps prickled up down Lori's back.

Lori paused in switching the laundry. Had she accidentally given the murderer the perfect opportunity?

Debbie had to have come to Dusky Cove late Thursday or early Friday. Obviously she hadn't stayed with Ray and Katie or Mitch. She still had friends here, but all of them thought she was dead.

There were only four places to stay in town: three bed and breakfasts—all pricier—and the motel. Could she have stayed there? Lori hurried to finish loading the washer again before she headed to her office. She dialed Walt at the Riverboat Motel.

"Riverboat," Walt's gravelly voice answered. "Can I help you?"

She'd tried to help him improve his customer service, and the greeting was better than he'd used in the past. "Hey, Walt, it's Lori. Did you know Debbie Watson Griffin?"

"Yup."

"Have you seen her recently?" As soon as Lori asked this, she realized how stupid it would sound to someone if they hadn't seen the papers this weekend. *Have you seen someone who died ten years ago?*

"Nope," Walt said. He fell silent, but Lori could almost sense that this was more of a hesitation than a pause. "But now that you mention it, there was a lady staying here that mighta looked a little like her."

Lori began pacing almost involuntarily, glad for a cordless phone. "Is she there? Did she check out?"

"No, she was only staying one night."

Hm. She couldn't be sure whether that helped her case or not. "When was she there?"

"Checked in Thursday."

Lori stopped. Could it really be? "What name did she use?"

"Lizzie Bennett."

She rubbed her temples. People could share a name with the protagonist of *Pride and Prejudice*, sure, but what were the odds?

Lori racked her brain for Debbie's middle name. Had she ever seen her grave?

The flyer Chip had given her. *Debbie E W Griffin.*

A middle initial of E, a wedding ring . . . had Debbie changed her identity?

Anything was possible. It wasn't as though she'd run away to hide in a closet for a decade. Of course she'd work to build a new life. It could have even paralleled her old life. For all Lori knew, maybe Debbie had gone on to have a family.

"Thanks, Walt," she said, trying to keep her voice even. None of this answered the most pressing questions now: why did that new life have to end? Who could have done this to her?

Lori hung up the phone again.

Was this her fault?

No. Of course not. There was no way she could have known Shawn would know Debbie—Lizzie—whoever—at all, or have any reason to kill her. She still didn't have evidence he *did* know her, just one bad, generic photo. And a hunch.

But all this time, everyone in town was so sure her death now had to have something to do with her life—and alleged death—then. What if they were wrong? What if it all had to do with her new life?

Lori flopped into her office chair. That didn't make sense either. If her death had nothing to do with her life here, why come back here? After all this time, what could have made her return?

Lori couldn't imagine, but she had a hard time putting herself in Debbie's mind. Sure, she'd had rough times as a wife and a mom, especially once Glenn was gone. She'd wished she could just run off to some vacation paradise, but she also knew no such place existed.

And why start a life over somewhere new only to make the exact same life for yourself?

People were comfortable with what they knew, what was familiar.

Lori sighed. None of this was familiar to her. Not even the things she'd really, really thought were.

Chapter 14

As per usual when she was stuck, Lori headed out to clean the parlor. It really didn't need much beyond a quick dust and dust mop, but when she was upset or stuck, nothing seemed to help jog her mind more than menial cleaning tasks, even ones she didn't love normally.

If this kept up, she'd end up beating the rugs before long.

The door swung open and in bounced the Besases. Lori smiled, grateful for that one ray of sunshine. "Did you have a nice day out?" she asked.

"Oh yes," Chelsea bubbled. "We can't wait to come back!"

"Well, I hope we'll see you again really soon. Want me to go get your bags?"

"Yes, please."

Lori retrieved their suitcases from the corner of her office and handed them over. Both Manuel and Chelsea thanked her and headed out.

If only all her guests could be that easy. No more murderers, no more murder victims, just happy people coming here for fun and relaxation.

Lori laughed at herself. That reality existed on the same plane as the perpetual vacation she'd sometimes fantasized about. Certainly not in the real world.

The door swung open again, and in stepped Shawn. The yellow scrolls of oak leaves on the wallpaper seemed to move a foot closer, as if the room were shrinking. Lori made an effort to look down, focus on what she was doing: scrubbing at an imaginary spot on the sideboard.

Normally, she set out a snack here for guests. But she'd been so preoccupied trying to figure out if this guest was a murderer that she hadn't set out any offerings today.

"Hi," Shawn said.

"Hello." Lori concentrated on a different, equally invisible spot beside the first.

"You seem . . . frustrated."

Lori let go of the rag and looked up. Frustrated? Certainly. But not by any cleaning conundrum.

There had to be some way she could use this to help her, though. What did she need from Shawn?

Facebook. Of course. "Actually, I've been working on my online marketing today."

"Oh," Shawn said in a tone that seemed to go beyond sympathy to *I've definitely been there.* "What's the problem?"

"I've been working on Facebook, and I want to start adding guests as friends, but I don't think it's working."

Shawn's brow wrinkled. "Why not?"

"Well, just now, I was trying to add you as a friend—if that's okay—and invite you to like our page."

"Sure." Shawn pulled out his fancy smartphone from his pocket. "Let me check it out." He tapped around on his phone's screen and then turned it to show her. A miniature version of the Facebook website showed with the familiar blue bar at the top. He pointed to the picture of her by her friend request. "Is that you?"

Lori glanced at the photo. Doug had taken the picture last year, after her makeover, and she still loved it. Didn't he recognize her? Was he saying she didn't look that good now? "Yes, that's me."

Shawn nodded and turned the phone back to himself, tapping the screen again. "There you go, we're friends now."

"I guess that makes it official, huh?"

Shawn managed a small smile. "Glad I could help." He drew a deep breath and released it slowly. "Feels good to do something for someone else again."

Lori studied him a moment. Who was this guy, and why would he want to kill Debbie? How would he even know her?

Now that they were Facebook friends, maybe she could find out. But first she'd have to get Shawn to move on, since she didn't have a nice, fancy phone that could get on Facebook right here.

And that would be rude, anyway.

"Any plans tonight?" she asked.

"Just one last quiet night in, thanks." Although that wasn't really the end of a conversation, Shawn took it as such and turned to leave.

As soon as he was upstairs, Lori stowed the dust rag in a drawer and hurried back to her office. She pulled up Facebook and found Shawn's profile again. This time, she could see everything: pictures, posts, links he'd shared. She clicked on the photos and held her breath.

The page loaded and Lori started scrolling. The first page held no dark-haired women, just Shawn out on the water in a little boat, or pictures of sunsets and mountains.

Lori frowned, but scrolled down to the next set of photos. No dark-haired women, just more nature shots.

The third page of pictures finally did feature someone else: a young, red-headed woman and a little girl with fluffy, strawberry blonde curls.

If Shawn had just gotten divorced, could this be his family?

Lori scrolled through the rest of the photos quickly, but found no more helpful pictures, just family and nature photos.

Her shoulders fell in defeat. She'd been so sure it was him— but she'd been wrong before. Very wrong. It wasn't impossible.

Lori clicked back to his main profile and started scrolling there, digging deeper and deeper into his past. Finally, she couldn't read any more of the words streaming by. She'd already dug far enough to find pictures of his presumably ex-wife.

She scrolled back up through the page, rechecking for any posts she'd missed. And then she saw it, six months ago:

*I know this is a long shot, but with all the changes in
my life, I've been trying to get back to my roots. I'm looking
for my bio mom. Do any of my friends have any contacts in
the Wilmington/Brunswick County NC area? I was born at
Dosher Memorial Hospital in 1975.*

Lori sat back in her chair. 1975? Lori turned twelve that year,
which meant Mitch and Chip and Debbie were around sixteen.

Her heart made a slow trip southward as the realization set
in. Could Debbie have placed a child for adoption as a sixteen-
year-old?

Lori wasn't sure if this made more sense or less. Was Mitch
or Chip the father? Did Shawn know?

And if Shawn had finally found his biological mother, how
did he end up killing her?

She couldn't process this on her own, and she couldn't rely
on "ifs" and "maybes" and hunches for something this important.
This was too important to bring up with Mitch or Chip without
knowing which was the father—or if it was someone else. So who
was she supposed to ask?

Lori's gaze settled on the wall above her desk. If there were
windows there (and in the kitchen, the next room over), she'd be
looking right at Dusky Card and Gift.

Right at Debbie's parents.

Surely they were the right people to ask. Lori hopped up and
almost ran across the street. At the last moment, she remembered
she needed to go around back and diverted for the back door. She
was lucky to find it unlocked and offered only a perfunctory
knock before she burst in.

Ray was at the kitchen table, halfway to standing, as if she'd
interrupted him as he was coming to answer the door for her. He
looked a little less cadaverous than he had over the last two days
with the initial shock slowly wearing off. "Well, can I help you,
Miss Lori?"

She gasped for air—then again, and again. She really wasn't
used to running like that.

The magnitude of what she was about to ask an already stressed and frail old man suddenly hit her. What if he *didn't* know about this? What if it wasn't true? She needed to tread carefully here, if at all.

Lori held up a *wait one minute* finger and tried to catch her breath—and collect her thoughts. She hadn't even brought food to soften the blow. How would this question end up? No way could this bombshell end well.

Baby steps, she tried to tell herself. She had to take baby steps.

Finally, she could take a full breath. "I've been looking at the case," she said, building very carefully toward the revelation. "And I came across something."

Ray stood again and lumbered over to her, his bushy white eyebrows raised and waiting.

"So, I have to ask."

He nodded for her to go on.

Carefully. Very, very carefully. "Is there any reason why someone adopted from here in 1975 might think Debbie is his biological mother?"

Ray skittered back a stutter step. Even in the dim light of the kitchen, his face seemed to grow paler, his age spots standing out. He rubbed a hand over his face and drew a breath, long and deep and slow.

"Yes," he finally said. "She had a baby, and he was adopted."

"He? It was a boy?"

"Yes. Why?"

Lori opened her mouth to respond, but then she realized how shaky that evidence was. Dosher Hospital probably had more than one baby adopted that year. How could she claim that Shawn was definitely Debbie's son, Ray's grandson? What if she were wrong?

Even if she were right, she'd want Shawn to be able to tell them himself.

"I can't say for sure yet," she finally replied. "I'll let you know as soon as I can, though. Thank you for your help."

Ray gave the barest nod and shuffled back to his spot at the table. Lori made a mental note to bring over something for dinner in a little while and showed herself out, though she'd barely stepped in. She hadn't even been there long enough to close the door behind her.

She didn't—couldn't—run back across the street, but she hurried the best she could, still trying to make sense of this latest development.

Debbie had placed a baby for adoption nearly forty years ago. And now he very well could be grown up and in her inn.

This also meant there was no guarantee Shawn had killed Debbie. He'd come all this way, searching for years to find his biological mother. Why would he kill her as soon as he saw her? That didn't make any sense.

By the time Lori reached the back door of the inn, her heart felt light. Shawn couldn't have killed Debbie. He wouldn't. He was looking for her, and he'd finally found her. There was no reason to think he'd hurt her. In fact, he'd probably want to help find her killer, once the shock wore off.

There might not be a shock, Lori realized, if his mother's death was the reason he'd been sad most of the weekend. But that was a big if.

Lori locked the back door before she realized she'd forgotten a very important question for Ray: who was the baby's father? It didn't really change anything about Mitch—that was what you did in those days if you were pregnant and too young to marry, and he'd been married to her for over two decades, so she already knew they'd had a relationship.

But what if it was Chip? Would that change things for Mitch? Could they be much worse than they were now?

Lori's happy mood had turned a little more somber. She needed to know who the father was. Short of visiting a daytime talk show that would devolve into the usual soap opera, the easiest route would be asking Ray and Katie.

She could run back across the street, but the first run had nearly killed her. It was the kind of question you had to ask in person. Maybe this was, too, but as a follow-up to the conversation they'd just had, Lori figured it wouldn't be that big of a faux pas.

She headed for the office to call Ray's number. As soon as she rounded the corner to the hallway to her office, though, she noticed something wasn't right. The door to her office was open.

Didn't she usually keep that closed? Lori bit her lip and moved closer—and then she noticed the other person in the dark hallway. She jumped back a step.

Shawn moved forward into the light, holding up hands as if to calm her. "It's okay, it's just me."

Had she left in such a hurry that she'd left the door open, or had Shawn opened it? Had he gone inside? This whole area was marked private, clearly off-limits to guests.

At the same time, she might have just figured out who this man's biological mother was. She wasn't even sure whether he knew yet. Should she tell him?

It wasn't her place—but then the person whose place it was, was dead. Could she figure out who his father was and get him down here to figure this out?

Besides, if she said something, then he'd know she'd been snooping on his Facebook profile. Surely that wasn't why he added his innkeeper as a friend, so she could dig through his metaphorical dirty laundry and not just the physical laundry in his room.

Facebook could be a double-edged sword, she realized.

And at this point, the silence was becoming awkward. Lori had to settle for asking, "Can I help you with something?" just to be able to say something when she really wanted to say *everything*.

"Uh, yeah," he said slowly. "I'm having a bit of a problem in my room."

Lori glanced at the ceiling. "*In* your room?"

"Well, obviously I'm not *in* my room, but the problem is."

"Sorry, I'm short a handyman right now, so if it's that type of problem, we might just have to make do for a little bit."

Shawn nodded, very understanding. "Sure, sure. I just—it's not a problem *in* my room, per se, it's a problem *with* my room."

"Oh?" Lori wasn't sure why that changed things so much, but she was sure that it did. A problem in his room could be anything—his own luggage, dropping a book in the toilet, depression. Not really things she could help with. But a problem *with* his room definitely fell under her purview.

It was entirely likely that any problem *with* his room would also require a handyman's expertise, but Lori felt compelled to check now. If it could easily be resolved and everyone would be settled and comfortable, she'd definitely take the chance. And if not, at least she'd know what kind of help to look for.

"Can I show you?" Shawn finished.

"Of course." Lori gestured for him to lead the way. She paused just long enough to pull the door to her office shut as she passed, then followed Shawn up the stairs.

When they reached the upstairs hallway, though, Shawn hesitated. "Uh, can I ask something weird?"

Lori didn't know whether to agree without knowing what "something weird" might entail, but she just waited for him to say his piece.

"I was just wondering—my room is so nice, very on-theme, and I was wondering—could I get a peek at the other rooms up here? If nobody's staying in them, I mean."

"Oh. Sure." She turned to head back down the stairs to get her keys, but Shawn beckoned for her to follow him again.

"Actually, I think this one's unlocked right now."

It was? Lori waited to see as Shawn tested the knob to the Carolina Beach Room. The handle turned.

Had she been so distracted when she finished cleaning that she left it unlocked? Lori shook her head to herself and made a note to lock that door on her way out, too.

She reached the door and pushed it the rest of the way open. "This is the Carolina Beach Room," she announced, falling naturally into her grand tour spiel. "Like all of our rooms, it's named after a local community here. This one happens to be

Carolina Beach, which is about ten miles northeast of us as the crow flies—but it's on the other side of the river, so you have to drive clear to Wilmington to get across."

"Ah." Shawn nodded, meandering further into the room, admiring the large wooden cutout in the shape of the state with a weathered North Carolina flag painted on it. "Did you make that yourself?"

"I commissioned it from a friend of a friend."

He turned to the large curtains strung across the far wall. "Does the room have a good view?"

Lori crossed the room and pulled the cord to open the curtains, revealing the Cape Fear River flowing past the front porches. "Pretty much the best."

But rather than an appreciative response, Shawn just craned his neck. "Is the view better on the porch?"

She tried not to frown but unlocked the sliding glass door and pushed it open, stepping out onto the porch. "See for yourself."

Again, she waited to hear his praise, and again it didn't come. She turned back to him just in time to see the sliding glass door slam shut behind her.

Chapter 15

Shawn flipped the lock on the door and backed away a step.

"Wait, what are you doing?" Lori slapped the glass, not hard enough to break it—was she willing to do that, when she wasn't really in danger—yet? "Shawn!"

He didn't respond to her, walking away to the door. Was he locking it?

"What are you doing?" she called again. "This isn't a good idea!"

Shawn crossed the room back to her. "I'm sorry, but you know too much."

He didn't look very sorry. And he must have been in the office. But what did he know?

Lori turned away, looking out over the view that normally she loved. This wasn't her favorite way to view it, however. The one problem with this view was that it was isolated. If they'd been on the other side of the house, facing the road instead of the river, she probably could have flagged someone down quickly. Here, someone would have to almost be on her property to see or hear her.

But she was going to get out of this. She peered over the balcony railing. The direct route was probably not the best way. She'd already broken one foot investigating murders. No need to make the rest of her body match.

Lori hugged her arms around herself. Winter was fighting back against spring, and tonight it was winning with the wind coming off the river. She didn't have many alternatives right this second, but maybe her best choice was to get Shawn talking, explain why he was doing this, and think while he talked.

What had he told her? That she knew too much? "Why? What do I know?"

"I saw her picture in your office. I saw my Facebook post up. Should have deleted it." He shook his head, his jaw clenched, as if he couldn't believe his own stupidity.

"So Debbie was your mother?"

Shawn only fastened her with a steely glare for a long moment. "My real mother was named Melony."

Lori noted the past tense there, though she didn't think that information would be very helpful. Of course he must mean his adoptive mother. "Okay, right, Melony, of course. So who was Debbie to you?"

He snorted. "Not what I thought. I wanted—I don't know what I wanted." He ran his hands through his dark hair and finally turned away.

If she shouted for help, Shawn would surely hear, and who knew what he might do then? It would only waste her breath. Even if she used her phone—she checked her pocket; it was there—Shawn would still hear her talking.

And he'd run.

What were her options?

Lori pulled out her phone and looked down at it. No, it wasn't fancy with all the bells and whistles of Shawn's, but it still sent text messages just as well. Text messages Shawn couldn't hear. All she had to do was keep the phone out of his sight.

She glanced back. Just inside the sliding door, Shawn prowled like a lion watching its prey through the glass.

Keeping her back to the door, Lori shuffled over to one of the rocking chairs and plopped down like she was surrendering to her defeat. She pulled up her contacts. Who should she call?

Mitch had no reason to come for her when she hadn't been there for him.

Chip wouldn't believe her if she tried, not even if she could text a message to Doris at dispatch. She'd already played the "we need you here now" card once today.

Kim. She knew everyone in town—and everyone's business. She was even on Chip's good side still. Yes, she'd been instrumental in one of Lori's investigations, but that murder had taken place in another town, so she hadn't gotten on Chief Branson's bad side. Lori pulled up her number and tapped out the painstaking text: *I know who killed Debbie. He has me trapped upstairs at the inn.*

She sent the message. And then there was nothing to do but wait. "So what did Debbie do to you? How could she have failed you so badly so quickly?"

"All I wanted was to know where I came from, right? I wanted a medical history, a heritage, roots. I even got one of those DNA tests, you know?"

Lori only knew DNA testing in the context of crime solving, but if she thought about it, she could see how it would apply to finding your family. "You didn't want a connection with her?"

Shawn banged on the window and Lori jumped, turning around in her chair. His fist was still pressed against the glass. "I deserve to know where I came from. Who my family is."

She nodded slowly, not willing to risk upsetting him again. "Did you meet Debbie?"

Again, he snorted, the derision clear. "Yeah. She was only willing to admit I was hers. Had like one or two things from the hospital—even my parents had more stuff than that. And then she was all, 'I hope you had a good life.' Ha." His laugh was steeped in more bitterness than burned coffee.

"I'm sure she'd tried to make sure that happened for you. She was too young to marry and take care of you."

"Yeah, well, she failed. My dad left the family when I was seven. All my life, I dreamed—hoped—wished my 'real' dad would show up one day, even just to play a game of ball. And that never happened."

Lori huddled against the wind and checked her phone for the second time. No reply from Kim yet. "That sounds terrible," Lori tried.

"You have no idea!" Shawn shouted. "And then my wife left me and my mom died, and suddenly this 'real' Mom and 'real' Dad are all I can think about."

Lori didn't dare tell him she was pretty sure she could narrow the choices down for him. Would he kill his biological father like he had his mother?

And why had he killed his mother if she was all he had left, after looking for her so hard? "So you met Debbie and then what?"

"I suggested Miller's Point because you made it sound perfect. We would meet, and everything would be perfect, and she'd tell me who my dad was." His voice faded away in the last words enough that Lori suspected they'd gotten to the heart of the matter.

She swiveled in her rocking chair to look at him, rubbing her hands over her arms. "And did she tell you who your father was?"

"She said she couldn't." Shawn's face crumpled and his voice almost gave out. "It wasn't for me to know yet. She hadn't talked to him and couldn't spring it on him. But I don't understand—I didn't—I still don't." He pressed both hands to the glass. "Don't I have a right to know?"

"Of course you do," Lori said. Maybe she could still talk her way out of this. Though if he'd killed his own mother, maybe she shouldn't hold out hope for reasoning with him.

She turned back, though she wasn't really looking at the view, and checked her phone again. No word from Kim still? Usually she responded to texts at world-record speed.

The sounds of gravel popping underneath tires reached her ears. Was this a guest—could she ask a guest for help? Or was this Kim or the cavalry she'd called in? Lori straightened in her chair and craned her neck to peer through the branches of the oak trees shielding the drive on the side of the house.

"What's—what's that?" Shawn left his station at the sliding glass door. Lori couldn't see very far into the room with the setting sun reflecting off the glass, but she assumed he was going to the window to look.

Just as the white hood of a car poked into view, Shawn reappeared, tapping at the glass door. "Make this person leave."

"What if it's a guest?" Lori asked a second before the roof of the car was visible—it was an SUV.

A white SUV.

Mitch? Had Kim called Mitch to help her?

"Make him leave anyway. Tell him check-in has to be late today."

Lori stood and walked to the edge of the porch, holding onto the railing so Shawn couldn't sneak up and push her over. Below, Mitch climbed out of his SUV.

"I'm sorry," she announced very loudly. Mitch looked up and met her eyes. For a moment, her act—her lie—became real. She *was* sorry. She'd given him as much as she could, but it wasn't enough. Of course that had to have hurt him. Could she blame him if he hated her now?

Maybe they'd both be better off that way.

Lori shook her head, clearing those thoughts. Settle that later. "I'm sorry," she tried again, "but something has come up."

"Is this our new normal?" Mitch asked.

"Make him leave," Shawn insisted again. "Or you'll regret it."

She wasn't sure the threat had any substance—but, then, he'd already killed once. "We had to move check-in later. I'm . . . still cleaning up after my last guests. They left a pretty bad mess."

Mitch frowned. "What? Are you okay?"

"Why don't you head to dinner first?" Lori asked. Using her body to shield her hands from Shawn's view, Lori held up her phone, pointing at it. Mitch furrowed his brow but nodded.

"The Salty Dog is good. Just over there." Lori pointed in the general direction, hoping Mitch would pick up on the hint that he needed to leave.

"Okay," he said slowly and loudly. "I'll be back in a little while." He walked to his SUV again and pulled out.

Lori had hoped Mitch leaving would help her relax, but it didn't. He finally had a chance to make good on his perennial playful promise to rescue her—again—and she'd sent him away.

And why? What was Shawn going to do to her?

She slid her phone back into her pocket and turned back to him. "How did it happen?" she asked. "You went to meet your mother and ended up murdering her? Sounds more like you lured her to her death."

"No!" Shawn shouted, then collected himself again. "It was an accident."

"If it was an accident, your first thought should have been to call 9-1-1."

"It was too late." He shook his head. "I didn't mean to push her, but she slipped over the guardrail, and then she was gone." His eyes focused on the middle distance as if he were reliving it, watching her fall to her death again. "I didn't mean to."

Lori nodded slowly, mostly just trying not to upset him. If he'd already killed one woman this weekend by pushing her from a high place, her position right now was not exactly an advantage. "Why didn't you tell anyone if it was an accident?" she tried again, a little more gently this time.

"It. Was. Too. Late," he ground out. "Besides, let her keep that secret like she kept everything else a secret from me."

Posthumous revenge. Lori offered another nod, but before she could think of where to take the conversation next, her phone buzzed in her pocket. She turned her back on Shawn again, slipped the phone from her pocket and settled on the wooden rocker again.

What's going on? Mitch asked.

Where would she start? *Debbie's killer is one of my guests. He's got me locked out here.*

I don't understand, but I'm on my way. Is the back door unlocked?

Lori let herself marvel a moment. Obviously this was a little bit different since she was in danger, but she hadn't been able to say that same perfect message to Mitch. She didn't understand. She still wasn't sure she wanted to.

But if she could help Mitch understand what she was facing

right now, he might be able to bring closure for everyone here. It would take her forever to text the whole story to him. Much faster just to tell him—but she couldn't call him with Shawn standing there.

Or could she? *I'm going to call you*, she texted Mitch. *Answer, but don't say anything.* She hit the button to dial his number and hoped he'd gotten her text first.

The phone rang, and Lori prayed Shawn couldn't hear. It was quiet, but it was hard not to be paranoid at a time like this.

Finally, the line clicked softly. No hello. Lori pushed the button to turn it to speaker phone. "Let me get this straight, Shawn," she said, loud enough for him and the phone. "You've been looking for your birth mother, and you came here to meet her?"

"I was born here," Shawn said. "I figured she lived here, too."

They could correct that assumption later. "But then when you went to meet up with her, she refused to tell you who your birth father was. Then you pushed her, she tripped over the guardrail and fell in the river?"

When she laid it out like that, it didn't sound all that unreasonable, until you got to the part about letting her death be a secret like her life and vengeance was his, etc., etc.

"Any questions?" Shawn asked, his tone sarcastic.

"Sounds like I've got it." Lori pushed the button to end the call to Mitch and hoped that was enough information to get a full handle on the situation.

Back door IS locked, Mitch texted. *Trying the front.*

Lori was sure Mitch would know to keep close to the house and tread softly so Shawn couldn't see or hear him. After a moment, she could only just make out the sound of quiet footsteps on gravel.

Time to talk over the sound. "I can't imagine how that must feel," Lori said. "To spend so long looking for your mother and then when you finally meet her, kill her before you get to ask her any of those important questions."

"It sucks," Shawn answered. "I'm not asking for your pity,

thanks."

"Oh, no, obviously not." Lori's phone buzzed and she glanced at its tiny screen. *Front door locked too. Any windows open?*

Of course not. If only she'd thought to put out a key like Ray and Katie had—wait, she *had* put out a key. She typed out the text so fast it held three typos: *theres a lockbox under the last rockr. it has keyes to the porch and this room.* The elation in her heart wavered a split second as she remembered they were in the room her guests were supposed to use tonight. Would she have to clean it again?

And then she remembered the more pressing issue of being held hostage. By an unarmed man. Who probably didn't have a plan. She shivered, but mostly from the cold.

"All right," Shawn said. "I'm going to get out of here."

"I have your home address, Shawn," she said, so patient her tone bordered on bored. "The police will find you."

"Why go back there? There's nothing left."

The irony was that there in Atlanta, he'd always been closer to his biological mother than he'd known. They had to come back here for him to find her. And to kill her.

"Don't you want to see your daughter?"

Lori's phone vibrated again with a text from Mitch. *What's the combination?*

Oh, that was a very good question. Adam had been the one to set up the box. It should be set to the last four digits of the incoming guests' phone number, but she didn't know it off the top of her head.

Visions of being saved faded, although Mitch could surely catch Shawn when he did decide to leave.

"My daughter is better off this way," Shawn murmured. Lori could just make out the words.

"Of course that's not true," Lori said, but her mind was really on tapping out a response to Mitch: *call Adam he knows here's his number.*

Within seconds, Lori could hear the low tones of Mitch's voice carrying from the porch below her. Not distinct enough to make out the words, but could it still be loud enough for Shawn to hear? Lori held her breath.

"What are you doing?" Shawn called. "What am I hearing?"

Oh no. Lori's stomach crept lower. If Shawn knew there was someone here to catch him, he'd either sneak out the back or keep her barricaded here forever.

"Nothing," Lori said quickly. Too quickly. "Why, what does it sound like?"

"Someone. Talking." Shawn craned his neck to look around, as if he could see much from behind the sliding door.

At that moment, Mitch's voice stopped. Lori heard the soft click of the lock on the lockbox, and the quiet clatter of opening the lid. She knew that sound perfectly—it had woken her up at night often enough.

"Wait a minute," Shawn said. "How do you know so much about this?"

"Do I?"

"You had her picture in your office. You were snooping on me. Who was she to you?"

Lori contemplated lying to keep him distracted, but surely she didn't have to resort to that. "I didn't know her. I only moved here a couple years ago."

She neglected to keep the "buuut" out of her cadence.

So Shawn said it for her. "But . . . ?"

"I know her parents. And her husband. Ex-husband," she supposed.

Any moment he should burst through that door, and presumably detain Shawn.

So why wasn't he?

She tried to reanalyze what she heard from below. The lockbox lock, certainly. The lid opening, definitely. The keys being extracted, probably.

The keys in the door? No. The door opening? Nope.

Why was he hesitating now?

Lori cast her gaze heavenward. This was far from the most treacherous situation she'd found herself in—even with a murderer—but somehow she felt very helpless right now.

Finally, another set of quiet footsteps crunched through the gravel. Kim, come to check on her herself?

Of course. Kim had called Mitch to come, and they were working together. Mitch probably thought Lori wouldn't even welcome a rescue from him at this point.

She'd welcome a rescue from anyone. It was the giver that was the question.

But instead of the key sliding in the lock and the door opening, she heard . . . whispering? Nothing distinct enough to make out any words, or even identify the speakers, but whoever it was seemed to know about the need for stealth.

Finally, finally, Lori thought she heard the faint sounds of the front door swinging open. Finally. Rescue was on its way. She strained to hear the sounds of footsteps on the stairs, but obviously the chances were low from here, especially if these people were trying to be sneaky.

Lori was straining so hard to listen that when a knock sounded at the Carolina Beach Room door, she jumped. Shawn did too, pivoting to see who was at the door.

No one yet. Didn't they have the room key? Lori got up from the chair, no longer worried Shawn might see her phone, and walked up to the glass door to watch.

Shawn glanced back at Lori, like she had some control of what was happening here. Or any idea. She shrugged.

"Shawn, right?" Lori could barely hear Mitch's voice through the door. "I have something important to talk to you about."

"It can wait. Back away, or . . . else." The threat was even weaker than his words.

."Listen, I was married to Debbie. I knew her, I've known her since we were kids."

Shawn strode across the room and yanked the door open. "You knew her?"

"Since we were born, practically."

Lori knocked on the glass, trying to remind Mitch there was something they needed to take care of first—getting her out of this trap. Mitch nodded to her but spoke to Shawn. "Can we let Lori back inside and then talk about this?"

"About what?" Shawn was hedging his bets, it sounded like.

"I know she was your mother." Even without Shawn's permission, Mitch began to edge toward the sliding glass door.

"You don't know." Shawn shook his head, turning away from Mitch. "I'm never going to know who my father is. Even her husband doesn't know—the man she's lived with for, like, thirty years."

Mitch reached the doors and flipped the lock. He and Lori both pulled on the handles to let her back in. Then Mitch turned to Shawn. "Wrong on a couple counts, there, buddy. Number one, she left me ten years ago."

Shawn stopped short and turned back to him. "Oh. I didn't . . . sorry."

Mitch left the complicated history at that. "Number two, I do know who your father is."

The room fell silent, the air thick and oppressive. Shawn took a deep breath before he ventured to speak. "Are . . . are you my father?"

No. This meant he had to be. Didn't it? Lori couldn't seem to draw a breath, let alone try to run through the logic of the whole thing.

Two more seconds of heavy silence slithered by before Mitch finally answered. "No."

And then he nodded at the door.

Where Chip—Chief Branson—stood.

Oh. Lori instantly deflated. She was sure they were about to reveal Shawn's father, and instead, Mitch had called in the chief to arrest Debbie's murderer. That was a good call, too, but now Lori really wanted to know who Debbie had had a child with.

Chip stepped forward. "Hi," he said. "Chip Branson." And that was all he said. His voice, and even his stance, somehow seemed tentative.

Was this the same police chief she'd fought with for so many years? Lori was hard pressed not to marvel aloud at his transformation.

"Are—did you have a baby with Debbie Watson in 1975?" Shawn ventured.

Lori looked back and forth between Shawn and Chip, faster and faster. Wait, wasn't he here to arrest him?

"Yes," Chip finally said. "And we placed him for adoption."

Somewhere inside, Lori had known that Mitch and Chip were the only two reasonable options for Shawn's father. But to see Chip admit this in front of the man who was his son—who'd killed the love of Chip's life—she was stunned, and that was all she could say.

Then she noticed the tears glistening in Chip's and Shawn's eyes. After all of Shawn's searching, he'd found both his biological parents.

There was the inconvenient detail that he'd killed one of them and the other was going to have to arrest him for it any minute now. . . .

"What happened when you met Debbie?" Chip asked, his voice near to breaking.

"She wouldn't tell me who you were. Said she couldn't spring this on you." Shawn glanced at Mitch. "Sorry."

"It's a little more complicated than I let on," Mitch admitted. "We'll explain it all later." "But when you met Debbie . . . ?" Chip asked again.

"I was just . . . frustrated and angry. I'd searched so long and finally tracked her down here, and now she was the only thing standing between me and knowing my father, and I just gave her one push—one push—and she fell over the guardrail."

Chip nodded. "Shawn, I'm so sorry."

Shawn wiped away tears. "It's been awful."

Lori managed not to scoff. Certainly the last few days had been terrible for him, but he should have tried living through them in the shoes of anyone else in the room.

"I'm sure. But I'm also sorry because I'm the chief of police."

Shawn froze. "You can't—that's entrapment. You have to have read me my rights first."

Chip raised a doubtful eyebrow. "You're not a criminal lawyer, are you." His tone made it clear it wasn't a question.

Lori didn't know the intricacies of the law, but she hoped Chip did. Chip reached behind him and pulled out a pair of handcuffs. "The good news is that you've still got all your grandparents here in town, and I'm sure we'll all come to visit you."

Shawn hung his head and allowed Chip to handcuff him. He quickly marched him out of the room and out of the inn.

She'd done it. She'd found the man who'd killed Debbie.

And, in turn, opened a veritable case of worms.

Chapter 16

Lori stood a few feet from Mitch, still not quite daring to look at him. "Did you call him?"

"Yeah."

"Did you already know about their baby?"

Mitch hesitated, and Lori looked up. "They were pretty good at hiding it at the time. I found his birth certificate. A couple weeks before she left."

She cringed. That didn't sound like it had gone well, then. "Thank you for your help. And for calling Chip. I don't think he would have answered if it'd been me calling."

Mitch chuckled. "No, it didn't sound like he was very happy to hear from me, either, though."

"So. Debbie and Chip had a baby." The implications seemed to spin wider and wider the longer she sat with this knowledge. "How will Ray and Katie take this?"

"No matter who killed her, it was going to be hard. But I imagine they might be glad to know Shawn is around. Maybe. Or maybe they'll hate him forever and never speak to him again."

Lori winced. "I'm sorry I haven't been there like I should have been."

"What—oh, I wasn't trying to say anything. I understand." Mitch stepped closer. "I can go now, if you want."

"I don't know what I want," she admitted. "I wasn't even sure whether I believed you were innocent. I mean, I did, but . . . I doubted."

"Sometimes, I did too. Or I at least thought I deserved to be there for this."

Lori met his eyes, still full of pain. "You didn't kill her. She chose to leave."

"I could have done more."

"Couldn't we all? I could have done more for you too."

Mitch huffed out half a laugh and looked away. "I didn't expect that of you. Not after what I did to you. I wanted—I never wanted it to come to this. That whole first year, I thought everything was perfect. This was the perfect answer. I wanted more because I loved you—I still love you—but I knew we couldn't."

Lori hugged herself. Somehow, this confession, though it might not quite cover illegal activity, hurt much worse than any other she'd elicited.

"And then when you changed your hair and clothes, I couldn't pretend anymore. I couldn't tell myself I wasn't in love with you. I wanted more, but I knew we couldn't."

That painful time was still seared into her memory too, when Mitch rejected her, trying to say he just wanted them to be friends and hang out. She'd had too much self-respect to settle for that, so she'd sent him on his way.

And then a couple months later, he'd come crawling back, ready for a relationship. "What changed your mind?"

"I talked to a lawyer. We came up with a plan: we'd try to serve her with divorce papers, and if we couldn't find her, we'd have her officially declared dead. I should have waited until all that was finalized, but . . . I loved you too much." He turned away, rubbing his face. "I'm so sorry."

"For loving me?"

"For lying to you. I just . . . didn't know what to say. I still don't."

Lori drew in a deep breath and sighed it out. "I don't either. I'm still angry."

"I understand." After a second, Mitch turned and started for the door.

"But I still love you too," Lori admitted.

Mitch stopped and turned back to her. "Can—do you think we could start over?"

"Start over?" Hadn't they already done that, when he'd freaked out after her makeover last year? "Again?"

He shook his head, turning away again. "Sorry, stupid idea."

"No, no, it's not stupid. I mean, we can give it a try." Lori offered a hand. "Hi, I'm Lori."

"Mitch." He shook her hand. "Nice place you've got here."

"Upkeep is a nightmare. We practically had a handyman on staff for a while."

He laughed. Okay, it seemed teasing wasn't off-limits. "Can I ask you a personal question?" Lori asked.

Mitch visibly braced himself but nodded.

"You're not married, are you?"

He relaxed, but only a hair. "No, due to some recent developments, I'm not."

"Sorry to hear that."

"You know what? I'm not. I'd lived trapped by the past for a long time and let it rule my life. Made a bunch of choices I regret because of it. I wish it hadn't ended the way it did, but I'm glad I can close that chapter of my life. I'm really looking forward to the next one."

Lori met his eyes and allowed herself a smile. "You know what? So am I."

Lori Marie Barnes Keyes

and

Mitchell Herbert Griffin

request the honor of your presence
(not presents!)
at their wedding.

Saturday, December first
Mayweather House
301 Front Street
Dusky Cove, North Carolina

Dear Reader,

Thank you so much for reading Inn Danger! I'm excited to share this cozy mystery with you. I have lots more planned for the rest of Dusky Cove, so I hope you can join me for all their adventures!

Do you know the best way to thank an author when you enjoy a book? We do love getting notes from happy readers, but even more helpful is leaving a review online on Amazon or Goodreads. Reviews also help writers get advertising spots and spread the word about a book — and they can even help people decide to buy it!

Until my next book comes out, I'd like to invite you to join my mailing group! I've got lots of fun bonuses there, from recipes from this book to a tourist's guide to Dusky Cove. Join me here: http://DiDavisauthor.com/newsletter/

Thanks again for reading, and I hope to see you in Dusky Cove again soon!

Love,

Acknowledgements

As always, many thanks go to my beta readers, Diana and Stacey, whose feedback always helps me make my books better. A special round of thanks goes to my proofreader, Sally Johnson, who is an excellent editor and an even better friend.

Once again, I'm grateful to God for giving me this gift, a passion for writing, and reminding me not to hide it under a bushel.

And I'm grateful to you, reader, for joining me again in Dusky Cove!

About the Author

Di Davis was born and raised in North Carolina. (Unfortunately, not in Dusky Cove—it's a fictional town, after all!)

Her mom got her hooked on cozy mysteries from a young age. Lillian Jackson Braun's classic Cat Who... series are some of her favorites.

Di has been writing since she was a teenager. She makes her home with her husband and children in the Rocky Mountains now, so writing about Dusky Cove is one of her favorite ways to connect with a little taste of home.

Di loves to hear from readers! You can reach her at Didavisauthor@gmail.com.

www.ingramcontent.com/pod-product-compliance
Lightning Source LLC
Chambersburg PA
CBHW051241170626
46809CB00004B/1426